RUTHLESS PRINCE

BRATVA ROYALTY
BOOK 3

CARINA BLAKE

THE STEELE PRESS

Forbidden yet always mine.

We grew up together—our parents family friends, her father my godfather—so she wasn't meant to be mine. Too young, too untouchable, but it didn't matter because for so long I knew it was etched in my blood that Natalya was mine. It might be forbidden for now, but soon the wait will be over. Unfortunately, life doesn't work that way, and fools are willing to play dangerous games to keep her from me.

I fell in love with a man who thought of me as a child. Then I tried to seduce him, so he sent me off with a warning to not mess with a dangerous man because next time, he'd teach me a lesson I soon wouldn't forget. Unfortunately, he had no idea that I wanted him so much that I wanted that lesson. Family friend or not, I wanted Ilya in ways that he didn't understand. My heart ached when he went away, leaving me with only a promise to return in a year, but he broke it along with my heart.

CHAPTER
ONE

ILYA

UNCEREMONIOUSLY STORMING INTO HIS OFFICE, I toss the invitation onto my father's desk. It's the one addressed directly to me that I'd been holding on to for over two weeks, trying to decide how to react or even respond. My father had already told them we'd all be in attendance, answering for all of us as the head of the house—and the family.

"Well, good morning, Ilya," he greets me with a smirk, assessing me as I stand before him. He points to the chair in front of his desk. "Sit, my son." There is no anger in his tone, but I understand that it's not a request.

I take the seat like I'm instructed because I don't defy my father, and I came for his counsel and support even though I stormed in here so disrespectfully.

"Father, must we attend this event?" I growl, running my hand over my face after taking a seat in front of his desk, sounding more like a petulant child than the man of power I was becoming. The more I consider my

1

behavior, the more the shame sets in. Still, it doesn't change my sentiment on the matter.

The entire situation is totally unacceptable to me. At twenty-three, I have plans that don't involve traveling to America to sit around like an old man and watch a spoiled princess in her bikini, tits bouncing, around the pool all day for every cock in the place to see.

Fuck. I try to block the mental image from my brain, but here it comes, involuntarily. Natalya's lush curves on her slender frame invade my mind again. She's growing up too fast, too soon, and it's sinful where my mind always goes when it comes to her. I've been fighting these twisted emotions for a while now, and it's futile.

"Yes, Ilya. You may be a grown man, but Drago will see it as an insult if you don't attend his daughter's birthday celebration." After all, Drago Romanov is my godfather, and Rosalyn is my godmother. They're wonderful, and I've learned so much from him personally. He's taught me to be ruthless, more so than my father. "Besides, Rosalyn put a great deal of work into the event and expects us to attend since we will be in town." Damn them. I bet my mother set this trip up on purpose to coincide with their party.

"It's not a special birthday, Father. She's not turning eighteen, or even the special sixteen they celebrate in the States. Which, I may remind you, we attended last year," I insist, trying to find an excuse as to why it doesn't matter if I find a reason to bail. Although instantly, the idea of not seeing her up close sends a pang shooting through my chest. I could always see her another day when she's not dressed to garner attention.

"Da, but we must remember that they are our friends.

He risked his life for us. Drago is your godfather." I had not forgotten the story, and I hadn't forgotten how much their family means to us. He leans forward with his hands pressed on his blotter, eyes questioning my motives. "Why are you so resistant to going?"

I stare at this man in front of me, seeing an older version of myself and wondering if he can see right through me, but I steel my backbone and remember that as the future head of this family, it's my job to maintain control of my emotions and answer without giving anything away.

"It's the middle of the summer with a bunch of bratty children running around. I have no interest in dealing with that nonsense." Natalya's friends are certainly ones I could do with never seeing again. "They need lessons in manners and a bunch of sedatives. They're constantly giggling when I'm around. It's annoying."

"Understandable. At least Drago's boys will be there, and you are of the same age, so it won't be too terrible, no?" He tosses me a half smile, but I'm unable to read him. My nerves are frayed worse than when I went on my first mission. If it wasn't eight in the morning and I didn't have meetings to attend this afternoon, I'd pour a glass of vodka.

"I suppose you have a point there, although we don't quite see eye to eye."

"No, that's because Drago respects you too much. His eldest son is a bit jealous, but that will pass in time. His son is growing up to prove just as admirable and ruthless as you, my boy." My father smiles, but it doesn't reach his eyes. As much as he respected and admired his friend, he'd hoped to outgrow the Bratva.

3

However, our hands will always remain filthy, and I don't mind.

"Thank you." I'm proud of the man I've become. My father hadn't been the kind to get his hands dirty until the death of his parents and my uncle, whom he named me after. Then he ruled the light and the dark with power and agility, even if he preferred to remain out of the mess.

A light rap on the wooden door brings in a flurry of light fabric and a giggle. I stand up and greet her. "Good morning, Mother." She brushes her lips on my cheek and strolls over to my father before I retake my seat.

"Good morning, my handsome men." She smiles brightly, taking a seat on my father's lap that has suddenly moved from under the desk. "What is this?" She picks up the invite, turning the envelope to read my name.

"Ilya doesn't want to go." Damn, there are no secrets between them. Well, at least not the ones that are safe. My father does whatever he can to protect her, both mentally and physically. He'd never intentionally hurt my mother, who he worships. Between my father and godfather, I learned long ago that loving the right woman can bring you peace in all the brutality that encompasses our world.

She gasps, looking at me like I stole her favorite dishes and smashed them on the floor. "You have to go. Rosalyn will be disappointed if you don't. She misses her godson."

"Of course I'm going, Mother. I just won't be pleased about it." I suppose there is no actual way of getting out of it anyway.

"You will act like the handsome gentleman you are, understand?" she says, giving me a scolding expression like she has done since I was a little boy, but it's not her face that bothers me. It's the one behind her that tells me to behave. My father has my mother's back to the ends of the earth. What she says is golden, so I better do it.

I stand and adjust my suit coat. "Completely understood. I'm going to my estate. I have some business to deal with this afternoon. I'll see you for dinner tonight."

"Be careful," she calls out, always worried for my safety like the wonderful mother she is. I wave them off before twisting the lock on the office door and closing it. God knows they will be fucking in a matter of minutes, and no one wants to get murdered for walking in on them, or for any of the kids to be scarred for life after catching them fucking.

"Thank you, son," I hear my father call out through the door.

"Saving everyone else." He chuckles and then a growl comes, so I hurry before I hear anything else. There's no doubt that it was about to get hot and heavy because my parents are obsessed with each other and can't get enough of their love.

The thought of having that passion is one of the reasons I've waited for a relationship. I could have found a lover or two over the years, but in my position, I didn't want to risk screwing the wrong woman with connections to another family. A war or a wedding could be challenged just because I wanted to get laid, and that wasn't something I planned on doing. Until last year's trip to America.

Fuck. My mind goes back to where it shouldn't be
—Natalya.

She's grown up so fast. Too fast. Long, dark brown
hair mixed with her mother's soft features and her
father's temper. She is a natural beauty that nearly
caused me to choke on my drink that night—something
that hadn't gone unnoticed by my godfather.

Her sweet-sixteen party was meant to break boys, but
it nearly broke me. She was sin and a half in her gorgeous
blue gown that rivaled the color of her eyes, and I let
several wandering eyes force my hand. I should have
walked the fuck out and not taken her onto the dance
floor and twirled her in my arms as if it was an innocent
dance with my godsister. However, it was anything but
innocent as the sparkling diamond snowflake necklace I
bought her was resting just above her ample tits,
tempting me to kiss that soft flesh.

Then she leaned in with hungry eyes, pressing her
perfect, youthful body against me to whisper how she
loved the way I smelled. Her voice was breathy as she
uttered the words and my dick stiffened instantly, forcing
me to create a little distance until the music came to an
end. I hadn't missed the look of hurt that quickly flashed
in those icy blue eyes.

After that dance, I made my excuses to the family,
leaving to deal with a matter that had come up. It was an
excuse. Still, I made sure to make my time away count. I
had to let that pent-up *energy* out somehow, so I ended up
taking over an entire warehouse of guns from another
family who had problems with us. Once I ended any
opposition, I shipped them overseas for my own.

That night, Natalya had fucked up my head and balls

so bad that I went on the hunt for war, but one day, that would come to an end because the day she turns eighteen, I will be claiming her.

I shake that memory out of my head as I stroll into the hallway, stopping my brother, who looks like he's heading toward my father's office, just in time and warning him away from there. "They're in there together."

"Again? Damn. He can't stay off her." He scrunches up his nose and shakes his head. Misha's only eleven, so he has no idea what the hell he's talking about yet. Give it a few years, and he's going to want to dry-hump every damn thing that moves. The boy doesn't have any self-control or manners. I think it's because he's the youngest.

"Wait until you get a woman," I inform him. The thought of having unfettered access to Natalya makes my balls ache with need. As much as I must resist her until her next birthday, I refuse to resist that she will one day be mine.

"Look who's talking. When are you going to get a woman, or do you dip off to the club Petrov owns to get your dick wet?" My best friend owns lots of properties, including a strip club that he loves to visit. We might be friends, but we don't partake in the same activities, despite my brother's curiosity.

Pinning my little brother to the wall, I give the little shit a warning, "Mind what you say, Misha, or I'll pop you in your pretty face. If you're old enough to speak like that, you're not too young to learn a lesson in manners." I get in his face, knowing that he's pushing his luck and should learn to mind his elders, especially because I'm going to be the head of this family next year. My father wants to retire from the illegal end of the family and focus solely on his corporation, which is fine by me.

"Okay, okay. I'm sorry."

"Good. Don't disrespect me or our parents with that mouth of yours because if Father heard you, you wouldn't be able to sit for a week." He nods, and I set him on his feet before ruffling his hair. Besides, my wife hasn't grown up yet. Soon. Not soon enough, though. I shove him as I leave the house and climb into my waiting SUV.

"The condo." We barely made it out of my parents' driveway when I changed my mind. "Better yet, take me to Alexi's," I order my driver. My wife-to-be will need another gift, after all, and I mustn't come empty-handed. I sit back with a wave of calm coming over me. If I can't escape the little temptress, I'd better prepare for her.

CHAPTER
TWO

NATALYA

"DID you send all the invites out?" I pop into my father's office unannounced, which usually is a no-no, staring at him while he's reading a document.

"Yes, I did, my sweet. Why?" my father asks, looking up with suspicion in his dark, all-knowing eyes. Uh-oh. Am I that obvious?

I bounce from one foot to the other with my hands behind my back, anxiously hoping one person sent in his RSVP. He, above all people, is who I want to see at my party. Although, given our age differences and our last encounter, the likelihood is slim to none. "I'm just making sure we received all the responses."

"Most didn't send back the card. Sweetheart, it's the twenty-first century, and it's a pool party. Did you check with your mother?" he asks, trying to be polite while also a little annoyed by the unimportant question.

"Yes, but she said that some were sent from you?" My voice cracks at the end, and I almost lose my nerve and run out. Drago Romanov is intimidating to everyone else, but to me, he's just my dad until now.

He leans back in his leather chair, brow raised, and nods his head. "Oh, you mean your godbrother and the rest of the family?" He twists his lips while twirling the pen on his desk, staring at me. I can feel the heat creep over my cheeks, giving me away.

I don't want to make it obvious that I'm truly only concerned about Ilya's invite, so I smile and say, "Yes, of course. All of them."

"They're all coming. Well, I believe so. I didn't get a response from Ilya directly, but Roman told me that they were all coming." He raises his brow and stares at me. "Sweetling, do you like him?"

"No," I screech, answering way too fast, so I try to correct myself. "I mean. I love him as my godbrother, but...like, that's it. I'm going to find Mom." He shrugs and goes back to his document. I could swear I saw a hint of a smile on his face as he lowered his head.

I pace back and forth outside his office while I consider the possibility that he's on to me. He doesn't believe me. Oh, goodness. What am I going to do? Will he keep Ilya away from me? He'd never hurt Ilya because of it. What if he tells him? I rush away from his office as quickly as I can, hoping to erase that embarrassing meeting with my father from my brain.

When I think about it some more, it shouldn't matter if he tells Ilya anyway. Ilya thinks of me as a little kid. The heartbreaking, mortifying memory of my sweet sixteen still haunts me. I leaned into him and told him how good he smelled, and he couldn't get away from me fast enough. My godbrother was completely repulsed.

He left right after, and I haven't seen him since. Nearly a year, and there hasn't been a single ounce of contact between us. Normally he'd at least call for Christmas or make sure to stop by when we visited Russia, but he happened to be away on business.

"Where are you off to?" my older brother says, catching me running down the hall, hooking me by the arm to stop me.

"I'm looking for Mom," I say, hoping he doesn't sense my distress because he'd tell Mom and Dad too.

He smirks before saying, "She's in the back meeting with the planner, which means Father will be there shortly." The door to Dad's office flies open with a hard slam, and he comes rushing out toward the backyard without acknowledging us, his eyes dangerously darkened with fury.

"What's going on?" I ask Junior.

"The other planner fell ill, so they sent in another one from the agency. It's a man," Junior says with a chuckle.

"What? Are they stupid or something? That guy is going to be out on his ear or in a ditch if he makes one pass at Mom." I bite down on my bottom lip because this is going to ruin my party.

"More than likely the latter. We better break the tension." Junior gives me a wicked grin.

I stare at my brother and scoff. After all these years, I know him better than that. He wants to see my dad rearrange this guy's face. "You mean watch the show?"

"Whatever. It will be interesting either way." We take off to the backyard at a steady pace, but my father had a head start.

"Fair point."

Our father worships our mother, and her beauty hasn't diminished in all the years after having us kids, so men, and even some women, notice. When they make a pass at her, Father treats it as a sign of disrespect and loses his temper. The giant rock on her finger should stop them, but the bastards never learn when they dare to challenge his relationship. He's not worried about losing her, but they don't let anyone come between them.

Damn it—we're too late and we miss the show. The bastard is splashing around the pool, trying to scramble out, and my mother has my father by the arm. "Leave him be, my king. I've taught him the lesson he needed." My brow raises when I realize it was my mother that sent him for a dip.

"Get the fuck out of my home before you drown," my father says.

"I can't swim."

"Well, then, I guess you drown. Shouldn't plan pool parties," my mother says. My father leads her to the food tables as if there isn't a man in our pool about to die.

I'm shocked by her response, so my brother and I go over there and help the bastard out of the pool. We each take a fumbling arm of the man, but I find him too handsy. It's almost like he can't keep his grip and falls back in the water twice. We finally get his dumb ass out.

"Get out, and run before my father or mother grabs a gun," I say. My father has one on him, but he didn't brandish it. It's only because my father loves to wait before he kills his enemies, teasing and tormenting them before making them meet their maker. The soaking-wet fool dashes and slips several times as he makes his way out of the pool area.

"I suppose the fucker could swim well enough," my father grumbles, watching us come over to the tables away from the pool, partially wet.

"We got him out. You can't let him ruin my party," I say. "Do what you do later." I wave them off and go into the house to change my soaked clothes. Whatever he said or did must have gone too far for even my mother, so I don't want to know what it was. It had to be terrible enough for her to react like she did. My father, though, is seething under the calm exterior; I'm wondering what's going on behind those eyes. Things aren't over yet for the planner boy.

After changing my clothes, I find that the pretty necklace that Ilya bought me is missing. Oh, no. I search all my wet things, and it's not there. A rush of panic and sadness floods me, as if I'm drowning. That piece was like having him with me wherever I went, sleeping beside me, protecting me. Did it fall off in the pool?

I rush back outside and find my father and mother talking. She's still trying to soothe him, but it's clear that he's seething with rage. In tears, I tell my father, "Dad, my necklace is gone."

"What necklace?" he asks. His brow raises and I recognize the tension filling my father, but all I want is my precious gift back. I have to find it before I see Ilya again.

"The necklace Ilya bought me." I rush over to the pool, looking down at the clear water that has settled after the chaos, and it's not there. It would be visible against the blue liner for certain.

My father takes my hand and then pulls me into his arms, hugging me tightly. "We'll get it back, sweetheart.

It's probably at the bottom of the pool. I'll have the pool cleaner check the filter."

I wrench myself back, shaking my head. "No. I know that bastard took it," I hiss, rubbing my neck and feeling a slight sting from it being pulled off me. I thought he was a little rough when we were taking him out of the pool.

"Your mouth, young lady," he scolds me. He brushes a strand of hair away from my face and then checks my neck with a sigh that I can't interpret. With a sincere gaze into my eyes, he adds, "Sweet girl, if he took it, trust me. He'll be dealt with." Nodding, I excuse myself and slink back to my bedroom. I sit on my bed, swiping my pillow and tucking it under my arms to cradle it as I cry. I feel naked without my necklace.

A knock at the door catches me by surprise. It's only been a few minutes since I came up here and I wonder if they found it that fast, but I doubt it. "Natalya, can I come in?" my mom asks. I swipe at my tears with the back of my hand before answering with a choked-out "yes."

She enters gently, closing the door behind her. My father's not far away, but she's not letting him enter. I can tell by the gentle command she gives him to wait.

"My princess," she sighs, coming to sit beside me on the bed. "We'll get your necklace back. I promise you. It might just be in the drain." She brushes her hand down my back, like when I was a little girl. The comfort is good, but it doesn't ease the pain in my chest.

"I love that necklace," I confess, sobs locked in my throat.

"I know. You never take it off," she says.

"It doesn't come off."

"No?" Not since my father had it fixed a month after I

got it. He said it was my favorite piece, so he wanted to make sure it had a good clasp. I wasn't aware that the clasp was faulty, but dad said the market Ilya had gotten it at wasn't the best.

"Well, I thought it didn't, but I guess you can break it easily." We'd been visiting his family and were on a nice outing when I'd seen the pretty necklace. It was more than I'd brought with me, so Ilya bought it for me. It was more expensive than I thought it would be, but he didn't think twice about the cost and then even put it on for me. I felt like I belonged to him that day.

"Trust me; we'll get it back. Do you want to tell me how you feel about Ilya?"

"What's there to tell?"

"You obviously have a crush on him. Is there more?" She gives me a knowing look.

I stand up, tossing my pillow onto the bed. "What's the point? He only sees me as his godsister."

"Does he?" she asked as if that seemed like a surprise.

"Yes." It hurts to let the one word slip past my lips.

"Are you sure?" She reaches out and takes my hands in hers, rubbing them.

"Yes. Of course." I huff, unable to hide the truth.

"How did you learn of that?" Does she think we had some illicit meeting that she's unaware of?

I take a calming breath and then confess, "When we danced at my party, I let my emotions slip."

"You told him how you felt."

"Not quite. I kind of told him I liked the way he smelled, and he couldn't get away from me fast enough. If that isn't enough to tell you someone doesn't like you, then what is?"

My loving mother reaches up and brushes away a strand of my hair, tucking it behind my ear. "I suppose you have a point, but, my sweet girl, he's much older than you. Too old to be dating an underaged girl. You're only going to be seventeen tomorrow. He'd have to wait a whole year before approaching you."

"It's not like he wants me anyway. I'm sure he's got women left and right. It's not fair that I'm not allowed to date yet." I pout and stomp my foot, not making a very good case for myself.

She dips her head and stares with a piercing, knowing gaze. "Do you want your father murdering any boy that breaks your little heart?"

"No."

"Because you know that's exactly what he'll do. Hell, he loves Ilya to pieces like he's his own son, but even he's not allowed to break your heart."

"It's just a stupid crush. It's not like I don't have crushes on other boys."

"What boys?" she asks, digging for more information.

"None that I'd tell you about so Father could interrogate them." It's a total lie because I hardly know any boys outside of family friends, and that's intentional on my father's part. Still, not a single boy I've met could ever match up to the feelings I've caught for Ilya.

She pats my thigh. "Okay. Well, keep it that way. You're young, and once you lose your heart to a man like your father, there's no going back." She kisses my temple and stands. I know there's no going back. I love Ilya Semyonov, and I don't know how to make that feeling go away.

My alarm goes off, waking me from one of the most intense dreams of my existence. It wasn't even close to reality, but then again, a girl can live in her dream land. My damn alarm continues to blare, reminding me that there are a hundred and one things to do for my birthday party. "I'm seventeen today; one more year to go." I sit up and rub my eyes, seeing the sun is already up. Standing and stretching, I turn to find a present on my nightstand.

There's a little note card from my father. *To my sweetheart.*

I open it up, and it's my necklace. My heart nearly stops because he managed to get it back for me. Tears fall from my eyes as I hold the box in my hands. Rushing to my dresser, I put it on and gasp. Looking in the mirror, I'm unable to stop smiling at the sparkling piece on my chest.

Suddenly, something catches my eye, and I freeze for a moment. The shape is a bit off, making it appear a bit different. Maybe the metal around the stone got bent in the drain, which makes me sad, but at least I have my gift from Ilya back. I run out of the bedroom, looking for my dad.

"Where are you going, sweetling?" my mother asks as I run in the second-floor hallway.

"Where's Dad?" I ask, coming to a halt.

"Right here," he answers, stepping out of their bedroom with a suit on.

"You found it," I squeal, throwing my arms around him. He hugs me tight.

He releases me and says, "I told you we'd check the

17

drain, sweetheart. The pool guy arrived and checked it first thing this morning."

"Thank you."

"Calm down and get ready for breakfast. We have a busy day." He's so right because it's my party day, and Ilya's supposed to be here soon. I don't hide my excitement, smiling brightly.

"Thank you again." I give them both a hug and run back to my room to change out of my pajamas. My outfit has been planned for a month, or at least the three I had in the running. I picked blue because it's Ilya's favorite color. It's a pale blue, like the color of his irises. They're a mix of blue with a few specks of gold. They're beautiful. I sigh, thinking about how many hours I have laid in bed, picturing those eyes looking into mine.

It takes me all day to get ready, and I'm shaking by the time the first guests arrive. Most of the guests have come, and I'm missing the most important ones.

"Hey, girl, you look on edge."

I fan myself. "I'm fine," I replied, knowing I'm anything but fine.

"Take a drink of your punch already," my bestie says, handing me a glass. I take it and gulp it to calm down. My parents made a non-alcoholic fruity drink mix that's fabulous, and I'm on my second glass because I'm so nervous. Now, I excuse myself to go to the ladies' room.

When I exit, of course that's when the Semyonov family arrives, and Ilya isn't with them. They apologize, saying they came in separate vehicles. I nod, but I feel my heart fall out of my chest, breaking into a million pieces. Standing in the kitchen as my mother escorts them out to the party, I promise to bring out more desserts. I just need a moment alone.

"Hello, birthday girl," a deep, husky voice says behind me, shocking me out of my misery.

"Ilya. I didn't think you were coming," I say without turning around.

"I'm a little late. We took different vehicles." I spin around and take him in, hoping there isn't a plus one on his arm. I inwardly breathe a sigh of relief that he's all by himself.

"What's that?" I ask, looking at the little box in his hand, which is on the kitchen island that separates us.

"This? It's your birthday present, greedy little princess," he answers with that upward twist of his lips, smirking with that smugness that makes me wild.

"Are you going to give it to me?" I challenge.

"I don't know. I should put it with the other gifts, no?" Jerk.

"Why? I'm not a child." He swallows hard, staring at my carefully chosen outfit for today. I've slipped on a white tee and khaki shorts over my pale blue bikini. I hoped this tiny piece would entice him to notice me enough to think twice and not forget about me when he leaves for Russia again.

"You're not an adult either," he responds with a snarl, and my body heats up intensely. It feels like it's on fire. I want to take off the last bits of my clothes and throw myself across the island, hoping that he'll take me like the Russian beast I know he is.

"Since you want to wait for that, can I ask you something else?" I ask, my voice breathy.

"What, Natalya?" He's growing irritated for some

reason and I'm not sure why, or at least I pretend to be ignorant. Has he always had that tic in his jaw when he's annoyed? I want to reach out and lick his strong, chiseled face.

"Ilya, will you give me a special birthday present?" I ask. His eyes narrow as he grows suspicious, as he should because I'm not a child and my request is far from innocent.

"What kind of present?"

"I want you to kiss me." That's it. I've gone too far, but there's no going back.

CHAPTER
THREE

ILYA

I NEED AIR.

I've ruled men, sent men to their knees, destroyed those who crossed me, and I'm ducking into a bedroom to avoid a seventeen-year-old girl. I loosen my tie, breathing as if I've run paces when that couldn't be farther from the truth. The kitchen is just a floor below, and the backyard is merely outside the bedroom window.

My pulse ramps up as I wait for the little thing to find me. I know she's looking for me. The lust in her eyes was clear the second she caught me in the kitchen, and yet I excused myself as politely as possible. Natalya Romanov is a baby still, untouchable by a man like me.

Any man, for that matter. I clench my teeth at the mental image of some young punk putting his scrawny hands on her precious pale skin—the soft skin that is bared to the world right now in the tiniest outfit that shouldn't be permitted. What was her father thinking?

My blood runs redder than the colors of my country's flag.

How could she have asked me that question downstairs? I shake my head as I try to push the memory away, but it's too fresh.

"Ilya, will you give me a special birthday present?" She's wearing a cute pair of tan shorts with a plain white tee and the diamond snowflake necklace I bought for her when she visited us in Russia two years ago.

"What kind of present?" I wondered what her father couldn't get his hands on, or maybe he had already said no. There wasn't anything he wouldn't do for her, so why would she ask me?

"I want you to kiss me." Fuck. That's something she wouldn't ask him for.

"Nyet." My answer was quick, and she frowned like she was going to cry.

"Why not?" she asked, looking up at me with eyes that could make any man crumble, but I wasn't born yesterday, and I wanted to live to see tomorrow.

I attempted to let her down gently. "You are too young."

Perhaps I let her down too gently because her sadness faded and wickedness crossed her expression. "You didn't say you didn't want to kiss me," she purred, leaning over the kitchen island, dipping her chest forward and revealing her ample cleavage in my direction.

"I didn't say I did, either. Leave me alone, little girl."

I stormed away and went straight up to this guest bedroom.

Has she lost her mind? Seventeen. Just seventeen. A sexy, voluptuous, plump-lipped, smart-mouthed seventeen-year-old brat who needs to be taken over my knee. Still, she is too young for me. My cock isn't in agreement. Since when do I care about laws? I care about her, though, and my godfather. Betraying him isn't something I plan on doing.

I take a deep breath and remember that she's not old enough yet. Raking my hand through my hair, I tug on the strands, needing to clear my head, but all I can think about is getting my hands on Natalya. She's not for consumption. Because if she was, I'd devour her from head to toe daily.

"Damn menace."

When was she allowed to grow the fuck up and get tits?

Her father won't let anyone approach her with an offer yet, but if I catch any fucker sniffing around, I'll bury them before her father does. I've had eyes on her even before I knew it was more than this friendly love that I felt for her.

"Ilya, Ilya. Why are you hiding from me?" she calls out while I hide in the guest bedroom like a bloody coward. Her voice comes off in a sing-song tone, playfully teasing like the menace she has become.

Fuck. Does she have any idea what she's doing to me? My dick sure knows, and he's all ready to let her kiss whatever part of me she'd like. I'm not a saint, but that's the one part of my life that I've kept clean. Now, this little brat wants me just to give in and to sin all up in her tiny holes. It's not what she asked for, but I know that I couldn't just stop at one kiss. Tasting her would break me.

"Come on, come out, Ilya. It's just you and me. Everyone else is outside." My cock swells in my gray slacks, stretching the expensive material, not something I could easily hide from anyone at the party—another reason I didn't step outside and hid up here instead. If her father saw my huge knob ready and his little princess trailing after me, he'd probably choke me, godson or not.

"Natalya. Go back to the party now before they come looking for you," I growl behind the wooden door. There's a thin barrier separating us and even thinner self-control, stopping me from forgetting whatever decency remains left in my bones.

"What are you afraid of? You're a big Bratva man now." She knows how to fucking push me.

I pop out from behind the door and drag her inside, slamming the bedroom door shut. Flipping the lock, I throw Natalya's petite body against it with her back thudding the surface. With my arms framing her body and trapping her, I stare her down without a word for a minute. Our eyes are both pale blue, but her pupils are dilated. I wonder if those asshole friends down there have slipped her something, or if she's so full of lust that she's let go of all inhibitions. Soon, I'll find out.

Her breathing is heavy, lustful, and yet there's a hint of fear in her eyes. She's bitten off more than she can chew, but she wants to challenge a man. A man who has become obsessed, aching to touch and taste this little feisty princess in front of me. So much so, I'd risk everything for a hit of her.

I grab her by the throat, holding her firmly and then lean in with my hips, letting her feel every inch of steel that she created. "Do you know what I could do to you, little girl? Right here, right now?"

"You wouldn't." Her voice shakes, proving she's not

ready for what she wants no matter how boldly she tossed out the words.

"Why not? You're offering up your pussy so freely to me. I kill people, Princess. Do you think taking your sweet cunt a little sooner than planned would bother me?" She gasps, eyes blinking wildly.

"My father wouldn't like it," she stammers out as if I didn't know that already. That thought may be the only thing holding me back. The devil on my shoulder doesn't give a fuck about American or Russian laws. I'm not American, and we both know I skirt Russian laws all the damn time.

"Exactly, and yet, here you are throwing your hot little cunt in my face, demanding I fucking taste it, eat it, fuck it, breed it. Are you asking for it, knowing that I'll have to go to war with your father over it? Ready to say goodbye to one of us or someone in the crossfire?" I say, letting my words have the effect I want them to have.

"Why are you so cruel?" she chokes.

I tilt her head and then run my nose down the edge of her jaw to the column of her slender throat. "Princess, you have no idea what cruelty is." With a shift of my hips, I take my other hand and cup her sex, feeling her heat. Massaging the soft material that keeps me from her virginal hole, I hold back my own desire and keep all expression off my face.

As she grows wild, pleasure rising, I pull away. Then I quickly yank her off the door with a quick slap on her ass. "Don't ever throw your pussy as a challenge at me again. Next time, I might not be as forgiving or law-abiding."

I walk away from the girl who had stolen my heart even before I understood it. When my protective instincts turned into pure lust, I knew I had to stay away from her, and now she's decided that isn't something she'll accept, forcing my hand.

I'm almost at the top of the staircase when I run into her mother. "Ilya, there you are. I'm so glad you're here. Your mother was looking for you," Mrs. Romanov says. "Are you feeling well?"

"Yes. Thank you for asking."

"Have you seen Natalya?" I hide my expression as best as I can, but her name sends me over the edge easily and I want to go back in the room and drag her over my shoulder right now.

"No."

She raises her brow and nods. "Okay. She must be around here somewhere. I don't trust that friend of hers. I think she slipped something into Natalya's drink."

I want to deal with the bitch myself, but she puts her hand on my shoulder, reading my mind. "Let me deal with it."

"Yes, ma'am." I nod.

She walks down the hall while I move down the stairs to meet with my mother who is in the same kitchen that my temptress had been teasing me in.

"Hello, Mother. Did you need me?"

"Yes, my boy. You disappeared, and so did Natalya. I was making sure everything was okay. Besides, you left her gift right here."

"Sorry. I had to use the restroom and it was occupied."

"Okay. Well, go find your godfather and greet him properly before I have to scold you again for your manners."

"Yes, Mother. Forgive me." I smile and kiss her cheek before stepping outside into the backyard.

It's been two hours and twenty-four minutes since I came back outside, and I've kept my distance from the birthday girl. Thankfully, the only guests from her school are girls because I might have had to lose my shit and been up her ass. Her father and brothers were wise to ensure that she attends an all-girls school.

"Shit, Ilya, Natalya's friends are all interested in getting your number," Drago Junior says. He annoys me intentionally. We don't get along because he's a pompous asshole who thinks I want to take his place in his father's eyes. I'm not sure why. I have my own father, and I'm sure once his father learns I want to drill their baby Natalya and breed her, I'll become unwelcome quickly.

"They are children," I remind him. The only one I care about has been avoiding all eye contact with me since she returned.

"Not all of them. Some of them are legally adults already," Natalya's brother says, winking at me like I'd be interested in a little dalliance with one of her friends. I'd never insult my future wife, but of course he doesn't know that I've decided to make her my bride. None of them do.

"They're all giggling like schoolgirls, which they are." I roll my eyes and finish my vodka. "I'm leaving," I say to my father, who is speaking to Drago, Natalya's father and my godfather.

"This too childish for you?" My father looks at the crowd and chuckles just as my mother approaches.

"Yes. I have matters to attend to whilst I'm in town, and I'd rather get them over with before we return to

27

Russia. Besides, I will pick my wife myself, and especially not from a pack of easy little girls looking to impress their friends."

"Smart move. There are many alliances we could make if you married one of the daughters in Russia," my godfather says.

"An alliance with a Bratva daughter might be for the best," I say, being careful with my wording.

"May I speak with you in my office," my godfather asks. My father and I head inside and then step into his office. "Please have a seat. Vodka?" he offers, holding out a bottle.

"Please." We both take a glass and let him pour us one each.

He takes a seat in front of us and sighs. "Yesterday we had a situation at the house. Strangely our planner couldn't make it, and a man showed up in her stead. Somehow, my staff thought I would allow this bastard near my wife without my presence. Luckily, I was notified immediately, and I went to check on the situation."

Both our brows raise up and we lean forward. "Yes," I say, waiting for him to continue.

"He let it slip that he couldn't wait to see the little princess in her swimsuit." I grip the glass a little too hard, shattering it.

"Shit, I should have taken that sooner. Here." He threw a towel at me that was kept at the little mini bar. I wrap it, but I hardly notice the scratch. My thoughts are racing. "Rosalyn pushed the bastard into the pool just as I came out."

"Yes, well, way to go for her," my father says, although I'm still seething, rage keeping me silent.

"That's not all."

"No?" I ask, barely getting the words out with my teeth clenched.

He shakes his head and pours himself another drink. "No. Junior and Natalya decided to help the bastard out of the pool because she didn't want her party ruined with a dead body in the pool."

"He put his hands on her?" I question, needing to know just how much damage I need to do to this man before I kill him.

My godfather nods and says, "He stole her necklace. The necklace you gave her in Russia."

"I thought she was wearing it," my father said.

"I knew it wasn't the same one."

"She didn't notice the slight difference, but I had to get a replica replaced for the night. Anyhow, I tracked the fucker down, but seeing as he was just at my house and everything, it would be too obvious if I did anything to him." His words are clear.

"You need to say nothing more. I will take care of him." He had added a tracker to the piece. He might be tracking the piece, but as soon as I learned he took it in, I tapped into the tracker as well. I wish I'd had time to add the tracker when I bought the piece. She loved it so much that I couldn't say no to her.

"I'll see you at the hotel," my father says. I walk out of the office and take my leave from the front door and not the back because I don't want the guests to see me leave, especially Natalya. Too many witnesses would make it obvious.

An hour later, I have my sights on the guy. The little shit had been driving an expensive car, and I was able to trace the pussy, James Smith, to his temporary residence. Interesting; he's not from here, but he's working for the Fratelli family, the fuckers whose warehouse I confiscated merchandise from last year.

This was about me. He came after my beauty in an attempt to get to me, but why through them? Was there more to it? Did they believe the Romanovs were involved in my bullshit? Either way, I'll deal with these fuckers.

It takes some planning, but I find my way into the residence without alerting any of the cameras.

The room is a mess, and it's clear he's living his life on the run—from the law, and now from the Romanov family; unfortunately for him, that included me.

He's in the shower, and that's when I spy the pills and drugs, and the one thing that led me here—her necklace. Problem solved. Seeing his phone on the charger, I know he can't hide and call for help, so I relax. Sitting on the bed, I pick up the device with gloved hands and check it, unlocking it easily. My first search is his call log. Then I move to his text messages. The latest one is from someone named Jojo. *She's wasted. The drugs are working. I'll get her alone soon. One of her goons just left. Be ready.*

That bitch. I can't send a message from here, but he's not going anywhere, so it won't matter anyway. I won't let him breathe after today, so he won't get his hands on my woman. I send the stream of texts from his phone to an untraceable cloud bank, then I wait for the asshole to get out of the bathroom.

He groans repeatedly, and I know that I've fucking inadvertently caught the fucker masturbating. Scrolling through his messages, an interesting one comes up.

Whatever is going on here, the man that put his hand

on my godsister and tormentor has to die. The second the door opens, I drop him onto the floor with my hand in his hair, doing my best to keep him from hitting his face. Can't leave him with bruises.

"What the fuck? Who..."

"Shut the fuck up," I growl, dragging him to his knees. "You need to answer a question for me."

"What made you think this was okay?" I held up Natalya's necklace.

"Where did you get that?" he asks.

"The better question is where did you get it?"

"I bought it off a slutty bitch looking to make some quick cash." Has this man lost his mind, or does he have no idea who he's dealing with?

"You are either stupid or have a fucking death wish." I snap my eyes shut, trying to control the rage because I need answers, but then he opens his mouth again.

"Neither. I'm not afraid of some two-bit muscle from Russia. You're nothing that my gun can't handle." He reaches the short distance and pulls one out from the bathroom, but he's too fucking slow. I send my knife into his eye. A scream rends the room; it's too late and he falls. I'm not going to get the information I want out of him, but I will make this work to my benefit. Turning the bastard on his face, it looks like he accidentally fell on his knife. Given the messy room, it's obvious it was a slip and fall out of the shower.

Ten minutes later, I made the scene appear like an accident, grabbed what I needed and made my exit without being seen. Next is a stop to return to the party. After all, I have to make it look like I never really left.

When I return to the gathering, everyone is getting out of the pool and almost ready to cut the cake.

"Ah, just in time, my boy," Drago says, clapping me on the shoulder. "Everything go well?"

"Not quite. However, I did retrieve the stolen item. He may have had a little accident. Showers can be slippery and dangerous."

"Da?"

"Yes. Unfortunately, I underestimated his stupidity."

"Well, we'll deal with the problem should any arise. Until then, let us celebrate, and I'll have to find a way to exchange the pieces."

"You'll have to clean this one. He had it with his filthy possessions." He nods, and we walk over to the birthday girl, who gasps when she sees me. That's when I spot the friend. Fuck, I almost forgot about her. I quickly speak in a hushed Russian accent so that only Drago hears me.

He growls and responds in Russian as well. The one I suspected wasn't the one; it's the other girl, the one playing innocent in it all. It's then that I focus on the young lady a little more and see that she's been nervously checking her phone several times over the course of half an hour.

As the cake's being served, I walk up to Natalya and greet her friend. "Hello. We haven't met, have we? I'm Natalya's godbrother, Ilya. You are?"

"I'm Jordan. Her bestie. We're in school together and like, you're so hot. Wow." I study her and the tells are obvious. If I'd given this any thought, I would have noticed the threat sooner.

"Thank you." I don't compliment her because I won't give her the satisfaction or risk hurting Natalya's feelings.

She looks at her phone, and I watch her swipe pattern as she unlocks it, although I don't need it because I have the number from the bastard's phone. All I need is Natalya's.

"Having fun?" Princess says.

"Da. I was just getting acquainted with your friends," I explain. She looks at me strangely, and I can sense that she's afraid I'm interested in this treacherous whore.

"Natalya, can you walk me to my car?" Jordan asks.

"I'll take up the task," I offer.

"I can do it."

"Nyet, Princess. You will join the rest of your guests." Natalya gives me a death stare, but she doesn't know what this bitch has planned, and I don't trust her because I'll snap her fucking neck and not think twice if she tries to harm a hair on my beauty's head.

"Do you have your things?" I ask the woman.

"I do." She doesn't even bother to say goodbye to anyone. We walk out toward the front, and I don't miss the eyes on me from my parents as well as Drago and his men. I'm certain he's alerted them to be aware.

"You know. I think I forgot something inside."

"What did you forget? I could have someone retrieve it."

"I'll message Natalya to bring it out. You can go back to the party."

"Nyet, no. As of today, you will no longer have contact with her."

"What? Why?"

"Because I know you've drugged her. I wasn't sure which one of you it was, but she was pretty drugged earlier. Luckily, I worked most of it out of her system." Natalya's lust definitely simmered down after our little encounter, and she was given water only by her parents for the rest of the party.

"You can't prove it was me, and you'll be in Russia, slagging off with your whores."

I lean in, holding on to the doorframe of her vehicle, and warn her. "I could snap your neck. It's the last warning I'll give you. Don't cross me because there isn't anything I wouldn't do for her."

"Ilya," Mrs. Romanov calls for me.

"Coming." I slam her door closed and walk backward toward the house. I see Drago's men watching the car.

"What are you doing out here, woman?" Drago snarls.

"Making sure she wasn't trying to seduce our young Ilya."

"She couldn't, no matter how she tried."

"Good."

"Did you learn more?"

"Yes, she's the one for sure. All I know is that she and that planner from yesterday were planning to kidnap Natalya." I showed Drago and Rosalyn the texts, and she gasps. Drago pulls her to his side.

"This is what happens when you want to be involved, wife."

"She's my daughter. This is the business I want to be involved in. Everything else I'll leave to you, but when it comes to my babies, I will never stop being a mother." She jabs him in the chest and then storms into the backyard.

"What do you want to do?"

"I'll keep an eye on her. For now, go back to Russia and play it cool. I have a feeling this isn't over by a long shot, and this isn't just tied to her friend."

"No. This is tied to the Fratellis and the warehouse I confiscated last year."

"Yes. They are after both of us. I'd say this is a distraction to whatever you have going on back home."

"I agree, but I'm afraid that I may have put Natalya in danger."

"I can protect my daughter."

"Of course, you can."

"Then you will let me do it, and listen to me when I tell you to go home with your family. I love you like a son, Ilya, but you know this is for the best."

"Da." I nod and go in and join my family.

CHAPTER
FOUR

NATALYA

DASHING to my bedroom before anyone sees me, I gently close the door so Ilya doesn't hear my chaotic behavior. As if I haven't already made a mess of myself in front of him enough today, I had to witness him flirting with my friend.

The first thing I need to do is wash my face so I don't appear so flush when I return to the party. It won't be long before my father comes looking for me. Running into my bathroom, I check my reflection and I'm shocked at how wild my appearance is, but it is nothing to the way it had been earlier when I pressed him to take advantage of me.

My body's still buzzing from the way he had his hands on me, touching my pussy, cupping it like I've dreamed about, so intensely, violently.

I panicked, but not because I wasn't ready for Ilya's touch. *No.*

I want him to take my virginity as soon as possible,

but where would we go from there? My hesitation is because my father would want to kill him. Ilya has had my heart forever, but that wouldn't mean anything to my father. I'm his baby, and that means no one touches me. Not even his godson, who he thinks so highly of.

I could have cried when he was all up close and personal with Jordan, getting in each other's space to the point they were nearly touching. Could she breathe in his masculine scent?

She's been so different lately, bitchy, rude, and then these past two weeks insanely friendly. It makes no sense to me. Now, she tries to steal the man she knows I'm madly in love with. My heart nearly fell out of my chest when he demanded that he escort her outside to her car instead of me, like he couldn't wait to get her alone. She's already eighteen, legal in both our countries.

Tears filled my eyes, so I excused myself and ducked into the house. I watched from the staircase and saw him leaning over her driver's side door, talking to her all close, then he couldn't even turn around as she pulled out of the driveway. It was all hitting hard and painful. He'd seen her and made a choice. I wasn't good enough, and she wanted him, willing to ruin our friendship. *Bitch.*

Eventually I shake off my sour mood because I won't let him ruin my birthday. For the rest of the party, I refuse to acknowledge Ilya, unable to peer into his direction because I might say something shitty, like how dare he touch me when he's such a creep on my friend. It's almost over, and most of my guests have left.

"Natalya, we're going to be leaving," Mrs. Semyonov says as her family approaches me one by one.

"Thank you for coming," I say, hugging each one of

the Semyonov family members except Ilya, who waits until last. He doesn't press for an embrace either, but my mother pulls me aside anyway.

"Don't be like that with him. You won't see him for a long time," my mother whispers next to my ear.

"Who cares? He's busy trying to hook up with my friends," I mutter as they make their way to the front of the house and we walk them out.

"Hook up with your friends? He didn't do any such thing. We were standing right by the front porch, observing the situation."

"Really?" I say slowly, taking a deep breath as I process what she's telling me versus what I could see from where I was watching from.

She squeezes my hand and adds in a hush, "Yes. We know she slipped something into your drink, making you intoxicated earlier."

"Oh." The color leeches from my face.

"Yes. So go say goodbye to your godbrother before he leaves." He waits patiently by his vehicle while I slowly work up the nerve to walk up and say goodbye.

"Ilya."

"Princess, I will not be staying with my parents in Chicago for the rest of their trip. I'm leaving for Russia tomorrow on business. I won't see you until your birthday next year." I let out a gasp, knowing we won't see each other again.

"Why?"

"You know why, menace."

"Okay," I say, feeling so distraught but remaining as calm as possible. He pulls me into his arms and kisses my cheek.

When he steps back, he gives me a warning. "Be careful, and stay away from that supposed friend of yours from now on. She's not what she claims to be. I promise you, it is serious. Your mother is right. She's dangerous." He heard our conversation. He tips my chin and says, "I cannot protect you from Russia. Please promise me."

"I promise."

"Good." I reach up on my tiptoes and kiss his cheek. He takes a deep breath and then walks away from me stiffly. Without looking back at me, he gives my parents a hug each and takes his leave.

I can't believe he's leaving and I won't see him for an entire year. What am I going to do? Why did I have to show my hand? Maybe if I'd controlled my emotions, he wouldn't have to stay away from me. My heart's already breaking. There are no words to explain the ache, knowing we'll be a half a world apart.

With all my strength, I make it through the rest of the party, saying goodbye to the remaining guests. After everyone is gone, I run into my bedroom and fall onto my mattress, letting the tears fall as soon as I land. There are no words for the devastation in my soul. Although, there is some consolation that he wasn't interested in her.

There's a knock at my door the following morning. "Sweetling, can I come in?"

"Yes, Mom," I say through my pillow.

She comes into the room, and I look up to see her holding the box that Ilya had with him yesterday. I'd assumed he took his gift back after everything.

"We forgot this one." She hands me over the small box.

"Oh. Who is it from?" I ask, pretending to be clueless.

"Ilya. He left it in your father's office when they were speaking, and your father forgot to bring it out."

"Oh. Should I open it now?" I ask, a wave of nervous energy washing over me.

"Of course. It's yours."

"Okay." I pull the little bow on the box and reveal a matching bracelet to my necklace. "Wow, it's so pretty."

"It's lovely. Maybe it's best that he stays away for another year." My mother's voice was far away, as if she hadn't meant to say that to me, but I heard it and my heart hurts because I don't want to go a day without him.

"What's the big deal? He is my godbrother, so he should be good to me. He's always looked out for me as if I'm one of his little sisters."

"Yes, but jewelry is special."

"Perhaps he's used to giving jewelry to the women in his life."

She lifts her brow. "Perhaps, sweetling, but he doesn't buy gifts for your other sister or me."

"Would Father allow it for you?" I remind her that no man would be stupid enough to give her a piece of jewelry if he wanted to live to see another day. Maybe my brothers could get away with it, but that's all.

"No. What about your sister?"

I arch my eyebrow and smile. "Well, that's easy because she's only ten, and Mrs. Semyonov buys Anya plenty of presents from all of them."

"True. Well, it's beautiful. Do you want me to put it on you?"

I scrunch up my nose and shake my head. "No. I'm not getting dressed yet. Besides, it's too pretty for everyday wear." It's really not, and it's as if Ilya intentionally picked a piece I could wear with jeans and a tee shirt or a pretty dress. The man had impeccable taste, or maybe one of his girlfriends did.

My mother gives me a strange look as if she's uncertain of my motives. Frankly, I'm not sure I can handle having his bracelet on me. Another reminder of him too close to my pulse, something I can see easily throughout the day. "Okay. Why don't you come down when you're ready? Most of the house is still in bed."

"Sounds good. I'm sleepy. It was a long day, and I want to rest a little longer."

"It sure was, my sweet little Natalya. Remember—if you ever need to talk to me, I'm always right here." I nod, and she bends down, kissing my temple before standing and walking out of my room.

Lying back down, I set the box on the nightstand and close my eyes. The best thing for me to do is forget Ilya even exists. I haven't the faintest idea how I'll do that, but I have to try. Unfortunately, my dreams don't allow that to happen.

A MONTH WITHOUT ILYA HAS BEEN TORTURE. HOW AM I supposed to go eleven more months without seeing him? Will he be here when the time comes? Every day I pace the house, wondering if my father will mention Ilya in passing.

Most days I don't go out. It's summer break and I'm going into my senior year of high school; I should hang out with my friends, but after my birthday party, I've been wary of all of them. I can avoid the girls until then. After the party, I don't know who to trust. Were any of the other girls involved in drugging me?

Did Ilya know more, or did he just see Jordan drug my drink? He couldn't. My insufferably handsome devil of a godbrother didn't arrive until after I had the drinks. How did he know?

It's been a month since my party when I get a call from an unknown number. I don't answer it, and they don't leave a voicemail, but then a minute later I get a text message, and it's from Jordan.

Hey, girl, it's Jordan. I got a new number. Sorry, your godbrother is a jerk.

I wonder what he said to Jordan that spooked her enough to keep her distance and change her number.

Yeah, he has that tendency. Where have you been? I haven't heard from you in forever.

Lost my phone. Had to get a replacement. Got your number from the cloud. Took me forever to get my password again.

I don't believe a word she's saying. She knows where I live and could have stopped by at any time. Something about the entire thing feels off, so I don't reply again. Instead, I tuck my phone in my pocket and head downstairs to meet my parents for breakfast. My siblings are sitting at the table, but my parents aren't there.

"Where's Mom and Dad?" I ask, pouring myself a glass of orange juice.

"You know…"

"Oh my goodness." I roll my eyes and then go to the stove where our cook is getting a plate ready for me. I take it, and my phone goes off again. My anger picks up, but I don't let it bother me. Ignoring it, I sit down and then talk to my siblings.

"So, are you going to answer that?"

"What?"

"Your phone." It buzzes again in my pocket.

"The damn thing. Excuse me." I grab it and holler, "What?"

"Princess, I didn't mean to be bothering you." My body nearly melts in a puddle on the spot, hearing his voice as if he's right next to me after all this time,

"Ilya," I gasp. "What are you doing calling me?"

"I didn't think it was against the law to call you."

"It's not, but…"

"I didn't say I wouldn't call you, Princess." I get why he calls me Princess since my father's known as a kingpin. Some would find it condescending, but I like it. My pussy throbs in the middle of my family kitchen with my siblings around. Needing some distance from prying eyes, I leave the kitchen and walk into the hallway where there is only one guard at a distance.

"Why did you wait a month?" I challenge. If he wanted me, he would have called me sooner, so why all of a sudden?

"What are you doing?" *Trying to fight my desire and understand why the man I've been fascinated with for my entire life has suddenly called me after running from me again.*

"I asked you a question first."

"What are you doing, Natalya?"

"I'm talking to you, obviously."

He growls, which sends a shiver through my body, and I turn my eyes toward the guard, hoping he doesn't notice. Thankfully, he keeps his attention averted. "Smart ass. What did I say about staying away from that woman?" I fucking knew it.

"I am staying away from her. What makes you think otherwise? Are you spying on my calls?"

"Don't believe anything she has to say." What does he think she's going to tell me?

"Don't spy on me again. I can't believe you." I end the call and go back into the kitchen to see Junior staring at me with a scowl on his face.

"She contacted you, didn't she?" he asks, and I wonder if it's because I'm angry or if he's monitoring my calls and texts as well.

I take a seat and try to enjoy my breakfast because we shouldn't let food go to waste, but my mood has soured instantly. "It wasn't Jordan. It was our stupid godbrother because he's spying on my phone messages."

"It's his job."

"Oh." I stab my fork into my eggs, losing my appetite with every dig into the soft, fluffy yellow food. "Why can't you all just leave me alone? I don't need a babysitter. I told you all I wasn't going to be talking to her." I drop my fork onto my plate, losing my desire to eat. With a scoot of my chair back, I slide away from the table. I'm about to leave the kitchen when my phone rings again, but I ignore it and toss my phone in my glass of orange juice. I can't deal with this right now.

"Nat," Dom says.

"Lia," my sister calls out, but I keep walking. I have no interest in talking to anyone right now.

I spend the rest of the day in my room, refusing to speak to anyone. I'm sure my father will punish me for tossing my phone in the juice, but I don't care. After the party, I didn't know who to trust, so I cut off all my supposed friends, and knowing that I'm being spied on, I don't want a phone they pay for. I'll use the money I have saved and buy a prepaid if I want to use one.

For now, I'll go without one. My parents are home, and there's no one else that has a reason to contact me. The only person I want to speak to is Ilya, even though I'm pissed that he's spying on me for my parents. It sucks that he's only doing it as an order and not because he cares.

CHAPTER
FIVE

ILYA

BEING AWAY from Natalya gets harder and harder every single day. Six months have passed since her birthday. I am halfway to ending my purgatory. The thought of her finding or falling for some young punk in the meantime weighs on my mind. Luckily, her father keeps a tight leash on her, and she's not allowed to meet a lot of boys. Most of them are during her free time, and even that is monitored heavily, which she hates. If she only knew the truth.

Drago informed me that Natalya was pissed about the phone and destroyed it. She purchased a burner at the mall the following day, but it wasn't like we didn't have the info for it and hacked it too. She doesn't use it, but she hangs on to the piece-of-shit device even though Natalya's parents gave her a new phone that she only uses to contact them. I don't like the damn thing because there are bad people willing to get their hands on Romanov's daughter.

I've restrained myself and controlled my urges, refusing to call her again. Calling her was foolish the first time. A rookie mistake for any man in my world, but the thought of her defying me and putting her life in danger when I am thousands of miles away is unbearable. The thought of something terrible happening to her is torture, and it lives in my mind every single day.

If I'd waited for Drago to call me back instead of rushing to ensure she didn't meet with Jordan, she wouldn't have known I was tracking her phone activity. Everything would have been a little more peaceful. Right now, all of Drago's men watch her at a reasonable distance while she tries to defy them at every turn, making things a little more unsafe.

Natalya is the perfect mix of her mother and father: sweet and tough, dark and light, and I want it all for myself. She'll be mine one day. I count the days, but it won't be soon enough. Every passing hour feels like an eternity and every shadow a potential threat.

The problem with the Fratellis almost disappeared from that day, which makes me apprehensive. It doesn't make sense to me that they would stop just because that one scheme didn't pan out, especially with that little drug addict. Something else is at play unfortunately, I'm too far away to dig deeper. My little incident has been ruled an accident given the fact that the hotel room had been messy and nothing, including the kilo of drugs, had been stolen. Drago was pleased to learn that there was no trace evidence left behind and the knife I left in his eye had been a standard-issue, everyday switchblade that was untraceable.

Even the Fratellis are under the impression the idiot

accidentally tripped on the knife after getting out of the shower. The blade even had a hint of coke on it from when I dipped my blade in it, so he'd stabbed cocaine into his eye, or rather directly into his brain. I wanted to check them out some more, but that meant entering dangerous territory. Natalya territory.

I head into my family home to visit with my parents and find my father and mother kissing on the sofa as always. My brother chuckles. "They never quit."

"You should be so lucky to find someone you can't live without," my father says, holding my mother close. My chest burns as I consider living without Natalya.

I swallow hard. I haven't seen her in person in six months. It's not that I haven't had my ways to steal surveillance footage and stills of my princess, but I'm unable to touch her, kiss her, hold her. None of that is an option for me until she turns eighteen and I can greet her properly as my future wife. These days aren't getting easier, and visiting my own family has become a burden. I've made my trips here less and less frequent, something my father has certainly noticed.

My phone mercifully rings in my pocket. "Excuse me. I must take this call." I leave the room and head out in the cold Russian air to ice over my heart while I mentally repeat *six more months*.

ANATOLY AND I MEET AT HIS GENTLEMEN'S CLUB BEFORE AS he had some serious issues to discuss and wasn't able to get away. Still, I hate coming here, but there are matters that require my attention.

I should be in America in two more days, so whatever it is, hopefully it doesn't take long and I'll be on my way to where I truly care to be and away from this debauchery. Finally, it's time to go to my beloved for her eighteenth birthday.

My best friend and I greeted one another at the door, and I'm led straight to his back office, away from the strippers who are in the middle of a performance. I don't give them an ounce of my attention because I'd never betray my bride.

"Thank you for assisting me," he says the second the door closes.

"Of course. Tell me what the problem is." He couldn't tell me over the phone, which meant that he was worried someone was listening in. Although no one can hear my calls, I wonder if someone is tapping his work or his home.

He swallows roughly before taking a bottle of vodka and pouring himself a drink. He finally points the bottle to me, offering me one. I wave him off because I just want answers. "Several days ago, I had three of my girls in the club go missing, and I haven't been able to locate them using my resources. Then, I received a ransom for them. They demanded that you deliver the money personally."

"Me?" Since when is the heir of the Semyonov family needed to deliver a ransom? A sinking feeling hits in the pit of my stomach, and no doubt a name pops in my head of who would dare make such an outlandish request.

"Yes. I'm not sure why you, but it's in the request."

"Who the fuck has the balls to make such a request?" I challenge my long-time friend.

"I don't know what the hell the Italians are doing

here, but his name is Nico Fratelli. War isn't my business, and you know I pay people to handle my problems, so I don't know why he's fucking with my people and involving you. He's got brass balls for sure."

"Fuck. That bastard again. I'll deal with him."

He tilts his head and sets the bottle down after pouring another drink. "You know him?"

"I sure do, and he has it out for me as well as some other Russians. Since you have dealings with many of us, you're collateral damage in this."

"Fuck. I don't have time for this. I'm a businessman, and I don't get my hands dirty." I look around this place and think he sure as fuck gets his other parts dirty. Frankly, I'd prefer dirty hands.

"I'll deal with him. Make the call and set up the exchange, but know this—he has other motives. He wants me dead and much more." He wants to destroy everything around me, including the most precious thing to me.

"Should I say you were too busy to meet with me today and give it time?" It's a sweet sentiment, but I'm not sure Anatoly is aware of how men like Fratelli or myself operate. We don't give requests without being prepared for those to defy them. Hell, I'll smell a trap waiting for me the second I head in to drop the ransom off.

"No, he's probably got you tapped and scoped out." Fucking hell, I need to get ahold of my father who will help me deal with these assholes, and I need to ensure that Drago has eyes on Natalya completely. He wants revenge on all of us Russians. "Make the call."

My phones are untraceable, so I send my father a message.

Fratelli wants me to exchange hostages for cash.

It's a setup, son. You shouldn't do it.

It's for Anatoly. We need to nail Fratelli before he comes after Natalya again.

We'll get him. Are you at the club or his estate?

The club.

Use someone else's phone and we'll track it. I don't trust this prick, but he's not going to get you. I'll slice him from head to toe before I let him take you.

Okay. I got it.

I send over the information and then wait for orders. Until then, we need to get to a secure location where we can hide out and plan. I send another message to tell him to alert Drago as well so that my love gets all the protection she needs.

We head outside through a private exit, believing the coast is clear, but we've been betrayed. Anatoly and I are on our way out to the vehicle when we're ambushed. I don't make it five feet before shots fly. The night is lit up with muzzle fire. My men are prepared, but it's too late because I've already been hit. Still, I drag Anatoly behind me as he scrambles for cover.

Unlike me, he is a pacifist. He owns businesses with his father, and this is just one of his many companies, so he's not prepared for this. "Fuck," he groans, and I see that he's been hit too.

I whip out my guns and go full bore at the bastards and unload until I drop them. We finally end the chaos, but the damage has been done. Slowly I try to stand, but the pain in my side and my leg makes it difficult. Eventually, I push past it and then survey the parking lot. There are bullet holes everywhere and bodies on the ground. There is one body that I'm looking for, but the bastard has disappeared.

Fuck. I saw him in my crosshairs, but the fucker played dirty and had someone cover for him as he darted into a running vehicle. I call my father right away, because fuck the medics. Someone else will call for them. "Pop, we didn't even make it out of the club lot. Anatoly and I need a doctor fast."

"We're on our way, son. Stay fucking strong." I hear the strength and panic in his voice. I wrap my leg, which thankfully isn't a dangerous shot, but the one to the gut definitely did some damage. Needing to check on Anatoly, I see his men going to his aid. His arm wound looks pretty clean, but the color on his face worries me. He's paler than usual.

"How are you, my friend?" I ask him.

"I want that motherfucker buried. Tell me he's one of the bodies on the ground," he says. I forget that he hasn't seen the bastard before.

"No, he took off like a little bitch," I answer with a grunt, my fists clenching.

Anatoly stands, clutching his arm, and groans. "Fuck, you're worse off than me. Sit the fuck down and let someone take a look at you."

"No, they're bringing medics in," I insist. My father has the best team of doctors just perfect for a job like this.

"You need to stop the bleeding, Ilya. One of the girls is a nurse, and she can assist." He calls for one of the young ladies, who is clad only in a skimpy outfit and carrying a medical kit.

"Nyet. I will wait for my father's doctor." I don't want

the hands of a whore on me while I lay dying. I should be with my love instead of this place.

He looks frightened of me; I would be too because I'm out for blood, even if I'm losing my own by the second. "My friend, you don't have time to wait." As the words come out of his mouth, I know he's right because it's too late and my world goes black.

MY EYES OPEN, BUT THEY'RE HEAVY AS FUCK AND BLURRY. IT unnerves me, so I reach for my weapons but I'm not in my suit, and I feel bandages.

"Mom, Misha, Nikolai, Mikhail—Ilya's awake."

I hear footsteps racing quickly, but luckily I know it's coming from my family. "Oh my goodness. My baby, you're finally awake," my mother's voice echoes in my ears, but I can't quite see her yet. I blink my eyes, trying to fix my sight. The room grows brighter and less blurry.

"Mom, I'm fine. I need to get up and go. There are things to do so I don't miss Natalya's birthday." My eyes adjust a bit more, and I focus. I'm in my bedroom, but I'm not alone. My parents along with my siblings are all gathered around. They stand at the foot of my bed as if they're waiting for me to pass on. It's a bit unsettling and I sit up, feeling the burn in my stomach and I want to vomit, but still, I push past the pain and the nausea because I have things that must be done.

"No, Ilya. Take it easy." I don't see my father anywhere around, so I wonder where he is.

"No. We're supposed to be leaving tomorrow," I tell

them. I can't be in bed when I should be on my way to see my wife on her special day.

"Bro, that was two days ago," Nikolai says.

"What?" A new feeling overcomes me, washing away the ills of my body: rage.

My mother squeezes my hand and says, "You haven't been awake for more than a few minutes a day."

"What? No. That's not fucking acceptable. I missed her birthday." She must think I'm not coming for her. "Did anyone explain what happened?"

"We can't. Not until the matter is resolved. With the rogue Fratelli member running loose, Drago wants her kept safe and well protected." Fuck.

"Please leave me. I need to rest." And to come up with a plan.

SIX

NATALYA

IT'S BEEN over a year since I've seen Ilya, and we're in Russia instead of his family coming to visit us. We're in Omsk, to be exact. We're not here to see the Semyonov family. My mother brought me here to meet men for the first time as husband potential, even if my father isn't ready for me to date or marry.

Up until my eighteenth birthday, my heart only belonged to one man. He had stolen it without knowing it. Then, my world crumbled when I learned he wasn't coming. It was what came next that annihilated me.

"Ah, that hot guy isn't coming this year," Rachel said. I ended up hanging out with some of my old friends, and they were invited to my party. Jordan hadn't returned to our school after the summer break, but I never asked my father about the details. I doubt he went that far because she slipped me some booze or something, but he is kind of crazy.

"*No. Ilya will be marrying a woman in Russia in the*

57

coming year." I'd been grateful that I had nothing in my hands, or it would have fallen. For the rest of the party, I pretended that everything was fine, but the tears were seconds from falling.

When I asked him about it after the guests left, he said that he wasn't sure who, but that he wanted to make an alliance with the daughter of one of the Russian families. I did my best, but my heart cracked in half.

From that day, I no longer wear the pieces he gave me. They are trash to me, a reminder that I am just a foolish child with an infatuation for a man who has no interest in a little girl.

Today I'm considered an adult, and my mother is taking me around to meet the best available men of our acquaintances. The Petrov family is the first, and they are well respected, wealthy with beautiful daughters, and I hate them all. Bitches. They're gorgeous and perfect for someone like Ilya. Completely Russian beauties; I'm only part Russian and not even remotely fluent enough to live here or be worthy to be his woman.

The day in the guest bedroom was a fantasy mixed with reality. I can't figure out what was real or what I made up. My father was pissed when he found out Jordan slipped some drugs into my drink. I don't know who told him or how she did it, but if it wasn't for her, I wouldn't have had the nerve to corner Ilya, and then he wouldn't have touched me. The pleasure was intense, even if it wasn't real.

However, I don't care about the pretty bitches; I'm meeting their brother, who is considered equally as handsome, although he owns a strip club. I have no interest in meeting Anatoly Petrov II. He's gorgeous, for sure, but no one matters to me but Ilya, even though I know he's an asshole who thinks I'm a child.

"Mother, I don't want to be here," I insist as we pull up to the gorgeous palatial estate.

"That's tough. It's time you met men beside the boys at home."

"Mother, I am only eighteen."

"Yes, and you've been boy crazy for how long now?"

"I haven't been boy crazy."

"No? Sorry, just Ilya Semyonov crazy."

"I..."

"Don't lie to me. I've been married to one of the most intimidating Russians in the world. I know it's addicting, but I want you to understand that there are other options." Other options? He was never an option, and that's the problem.

"I'm not addicted to him. In fact, I couldn't give a shit about him."

"Young lady, if your father heard that mouth of yours, he'd be angry."

"Where is Father?" I remind her with a tone I never give my mother, especially if my father is present.

"I sent him on an errand for me. I didn't want you to meet Anatoly with your father present."

"Didn't he set this meeting up in the first place?"

"Yes, but he can be so intimidating."

"Ugh. Whatever. If he can't handle Father, we're wasting our time." I roll my eyes, and then we exit the vehicle with our security flanked at our sides.

"Darling, no one can handle your father."

We walk up, and Anatoly smiles. "Mrs. Romanov, and this must be little Natalya. My, you are not little anymore.

It's a pleasure to see you again." Surprisingly, his comment should come with a cursory scan of my entire body, but he keeps his gaze focused on my face. Perhaps he's playing the gentleman in front of my mother. I've heard about him and his ways, so I'm truly surprised that my mother brought me here in the first place. Anatoly is a manwhore to the nth degree, and I don't want anything to do with him no matter how handsome he is.

"Thank you." I smile back at the handsome man, but I feel nothing when he takes my hand in his. Nothing at all, and then a chill runs up my spine and the hair on the back of my neck stands up.

A vehicle pulls into the circular driveway, and I don't need to know who it belongs to because my gut already tells me it's Ilya. I turn, and as it comes to a stop, he slides out of the passenger side sleekly, like a panther. He adjusts his gray suit jacket while his pale blue eyes remain trained on me. His dark brown hair is mussed even before he runs his hands through it.

"Speak of the devil," my mother whispers. There's a tinge of humor in her voice, and I wonder if she expected him to make an appearance. He walks up to her and greets her as he always does. "Ilya, my dear boy. It's so good to see you. We missed your annual visit." My mother hugs him tightly and whispers in his ear.

"Ah, my friend. It's good to see you," Anatoly says to Ilya, but he doesn't reciprocate that friendly demeanor. "Please, come join us for some tea, Ilya. Mrs. Romanov decided to grace me with her presence and that of her lovely daughter before our meeting. I hope you don't mind delaying it."

"It can wait," he growls, stepping in behind me.

My mother takes Anatoly's arm and has him direct her to the painting on the wall, leaving Ilya and I next to each other. "Please tell me where you got this. It's absolutely divine. I want a piece like this in my entryway." We follow along, but I can barely breathe with him so close. "Wouldn't this look fabulous there, Ilya?"

He growls behind me, and I can feel his head lift up in her direction. "Yes, it would look perfect under the stairs, Godmother." He presses his thick, meaty hand to the small of my back, leading me toward the sitting room. "Sit, Princess."

"I don't take orders from you."

"Natalya, please have a seat," Anatoly says. Now I sit, and of course, Ilya chooses the seat nearest me between Anatoly and myself, so I scoot myself away from him. He huffs and flexes his knuckles, cracking them easily.

"So, what brings you to Russia? I wasn't aware that you were arriving so soon?" he asks my mother, but I'm not sure I believe him. There's an edge to his words as if he's only speaking to be polite.

"If you remember, Natalya turned eighteen two months ago and has been eager to begin dating. I'm in agreement that she should consider her choices before getting married." She smiles the way she does when she's being manipulative.

"Yes. So, Anatoly, what is it that you do?" I ask him. A deep rumble comes from beside me, and I can feel my panties soak through to my pretty dress.

"*Anatoly* isn't interested in you." The thickness in Ilya's accent only adds to the ferocity of his words without him even raising his voice.

"I'm not?"

61

"Not if you wish to live another day."

"Understood, brother." Wait—is he going to marry one of the Petrov sisters?

He stands up and says, "Excuse me, Petrov, Mrs. Romanov. I must speak with Natalya privately." He takes my hand without waiting for anyone to agree, dragging me straight out of the sitting room. I turn back to see my mother raise her hand to our guards to allow it, and before I know it, we're standing beside his vehicle.

"Hello to you as well, Mr. Semyonov."

"What did I tell you, Princess?"

"I don't know. I was too young for you?" I sass.

"I warned you about flaunting your pussy in front of me again."

"Flaunting? How?" Has he lost his mind? I look down at my knees, which are pushed together, and you can't see my panties.

"You're fucking out here meeting with Anatoly Petrov for no other reason than a marriage option. If you thought for a fucking bloody second that I wouldn't know about it, you are wrong. Extremely wrong. There is nothing about you that I'm not aware of." He's seething, and I can see the color of his eyes darken with every word out of his vicious mouth.

I wanted him, but he left me and didn't even wish me a happy birthday. "It seems you weren't aware of my birthday." What kind of piece of shit does that? With the way he's acting, you'd think he would have beaten down my door two months ago when I became legal.

He's quiet, face hardening, and doesn't say a word. "Well, if that's all. I should get back to my mother and

Anatoly. I'd hate to keep him waiting. It's rude, you know."

"What the fuck is wrong with you? In, now," he snarls, holding the door open. I don't move, so he picks me up and places me into the seat as the SUV takes off.

CHAPTER
SEVEN

ILYA

I GIVE my driver commands to take us to my compound in Omsk because I don't want to waste a minute with my bride. She's asking for me to kill my friend, and right now, I'm not above it. The bastard enjoyed the torture, smiling like the prick he is. He called me the very second Mrs. Romanov said she and Natalya were coming to visit. *Asshole*. I owe him a bottle of my finest vodka as well as a punch in his nuts. It's his fault that I was in this position in the first place. She would have been mine months ago.

I'd been shot because I met him at his club, and I saved his fucking life. Unfortunately, his missing girls weren't so lucky. Fratelli and his men killed them the first day after violating them; it was just a ploy to get me out in the open. Fratelli's still out there, so I'm not sure what fucking game they're playing by bringing Natalya here in the first place. She is not safe until he's found and butchered.

"Have you lost your mind? My father's going to send

his men to look for me," she screeches, slapping my chest.

"I don't care. He won't do anything that could harm you, which means he won't use force." Although, I'm not so sure. He knew I wasn't ready to head to Chicago. Fuck. We had an unspoken agreement, and I thought he understood me. Now, he's put my bride in danger, and that's unacceptable. I'm not asking for permission, and I'm not giving her back. I'll do everything to protect her because Natalya's mine.

She freezes, a shiver of fear washing over her. "Would you hurt me?"

"That depends, Princess. That depends." I stare right between her thighs, licking my lips. My cock is going to tear her tight hole wide open our first time. The animal in me understands that I've waited too long to claim what's mine, and the buildup is insatiable. A part of me is definitely going to hurt her, even if it's unintentional.

"Where are you taking me?"

"One of our homes."

"Our homes? What about your fiancée?"

"My fiancée? Who the fuck told you I had a fiancée?"

"My father." I want to punch the back of the seat, but I can't let her see how pissed off I am.

"I told you that you're mine. I had some things to take care of and your father knew it, so I'm not sure why he would say something like that."

"Maybe it's because he doesn't think you're right for me."

"There's no one better. I'd die for you, Natalya." My mouth is on hers, sharing the kiss I've coveted for so long. She gasps, freezes, and then clings to me, pressing her soft lips against mine hungrily. Natalya flings her body into mine, causing me to grunt, but I bite back the urge to lose complete control. There's no way I'll take her in a vehicle for our first time. Later, when she's practiced, she'll ride my cock wherever we go, so when we arrive everyone will know she's mine as my seed drips down her thighs.

"I don't want you to die, Ilya, but it's foolish to go against my father."

"I'm not giving you up for anyone. He shouldn't have given you his blessing only to send you to meet other men."

"He gave his blessing?"

"Yes, and if I had arrived on time, our mothers would have already been planning our wedding."

"Why weren't you there?"

"Business held me up."

"Will business always get in the way?"

"I hope it never does again."

"You couldn't even call?" I can see the cogs in her head already turning. "Damn it, Ilya. What happened?"

"I was incapacitated, but that is all I will say. You need not worry because I am well now." Tears fill her eyes, and I can't stand it. I brush them away with the pads of my thumbs. "Please don't cry, Princess. You're too precious to shed tears for me."

"Ilya, did you almost die?"

"Princess, we have arrived." I take her hand and kiss it, waiting for the all-clear from my men. We have several on guard who have the entire building protected. There is no way for Nico Fratelli or his men to get in. No visitor that is unwelcome will be allowed entry, and that includes my godfather who has yet to reach out. Perhaps my godmother has yet to inform him that I've taken my bride.

My driver, Yoseph, gives the signal and I exit first, taking Natalya's hand and leading her into my property. "Will life always be like this, Ilya?"

"Nyet, Natalya. It was not smart for your parents to bring you here just yet. So I will do what I must to keep you safe." She clings to me, tighter than before and although it gives me pleasure, it's not the reason I want her touch to be so intense. Her tiny frame should be hanging on to me from pure desire. "I'll never let anything happen to you," I promise.

"Please don't say that. It's the thing someone says before the floor falls from under them."

"Very well. I will do everything in my power to always protect you and our family." I kiss her temple and lead her onto the elevator. The second the elevator doors close, I pin her to the wall. "When it comes to family, I plan on starting it right away, Natalya." My hand slides down her soft cheek. She closes her eyes and turns her face into my touch. Her tongue slips out of her lips, licking them lightly. "Fuck, we're going to be starting very soon."

"We've wasted two months."

"Little one, I shouldn't even have you in my arms yet, but they waved the red flag in a bull's face. You're mine, and I refuse to wait any longer." The doors open to my condo, and I carry her to the entrance table; there's no more waiting. Setting her on the surface, I remove her heels and shake off my coat. My mouth clings to hers, kissing her lips until she's pulling on my shirt, tugging it from my slacks.

I undo my holster and set it down before kicking off my shoes and then return to her mouth. Fuck, I've yearned for this woman for so long, I don't know if I'll make it to our bed.

Sliding my hands along her throat and up into her hair, I tilt her head to look into my eyes. "I'll be in between those legs whenever I want, so spread them for me." Her innocence holds her back, but my girl's eyes scream for guidance. "I said show me what's mine." She parts them like I demand, showing me what I've craved for so long, longer than I should have or deserved. "Okay, good girl." I press my lips to her forehead. "That's it. It's time for me to eat that sweet little pussy that I've been waiting for. You haven't let anyone else touch you, have you?"

"No, I haven't. It's only yours." Of course she hasn't, but I have to ask because I'm feral and possessive. I'll kill any bastard who puts his hands on my princess. She's mine, and mine alone.

Her dress rides up, and her pale-yellow panties are soaked just for me. I run my fingers over her mound, rubbing that tender spot, and watch as her eyes slam shut. "Open up those gorgeous eyes, Princess. I want to see you come for me."

Hooking a finger under the material, I push it to the side and run one down her slit. Fuck, she's so wet and soft. The squishy, wet sound causes me to grow wilder, moving faster. My thumb joins, and I massage her little nub at the top of her slit.

"Oh, hell, Ilya. I'm...oh my goodness." I push one finger inside, needing to feel her. "Shit," Her head drops forward onto my shoulder while her back bows, hips rock, and her pretty pussy clenches around my finger. "I'm coming."

I drop to my knees because I'm not done. Her pussy is only getting warmed up. Sliding her panties down her legs, I open them again and kneel between them. Yanking her to the edge, I run my face over her sensitive flesh. "Ilya, what are you..."

"What do you think? I've waited so damn long to eat your virgin pussy. I'm not missing out on this untouched cunt. Lie back or ride my face, Princess, but you will be coming again before I stuff you with my big cock."

Her already blushed-stained cheeks darken with embarrassment, but she leans back on her elbows. "Good girl. Give me that pussy and cream on my face." I slide my tongue along her gash, tasting her for the first time, and the animal who has waited so damn long has finally been unleashed Growling, I nip at her folds, kissing each one before pushing my tongue in and out, fucking her hole. Taking both my hands, I spread her open and eat my fill. My dick leaks cum all over my briefs. Fuck. I'm going to nut before I get inside her.

Her voice shakes as I roughly devour her virgin cunt, licking and sucking on her little nub that's hardened for me. She's ready to come again like a good wife, eager for my tongue and touch. "Ilya," she whimpers, fingers sliding into my hair, growing bolder.

"Good girl. Feed me your pussy. Show your man where he gets his meals." She presses my face into her mound, and I growl as I suck on her. My fingers pump faster, staying shallow because my dick will have the honor of barreling through the last vestiges of her innocence.

"Goodness, I'm coming again," she cries, thighs squeezing around my head, and I'd gladly die this way, but she relaxes and slides her heels down my back. "You're trying to kill me."

"Only with pleasure, but we're not done. I want you naked and with my cock buried in this tight little hole, filling your womb with my child." She gasps, heat spreading across her already flushed face.

Swinging her body into my arms, I cradle my woman close to my chest and carry her to our bed. Setting her on the mattress, I growl, "Take the dress off, or I'll tear it off."

"I'm almost tempted to see you try, but I don't want to end up walking around naked."

"No one else will see you naked unless they want to end up with no eyes," I promise. "Now lose the dress, Princess. I can't wait any longer." My strong, adept hands suddenly can't grasp my belt properly. She unzips her dress and stands, letting it fall to the floor, leaving her in just a sexy pale-yellow bra that matches her panties. Fuck.

"It looks like you could use some help." She reaches for my belt, but I swat her hands away.

"Don't you touch my dick. I'm about to fuck you like a rabid animal."

She licks her lips and pops the clasp on the back of her bra, revealing her breasts to me slowly as it falls. Natalya smiles, enjoying the sexy torture she's inflicting on me while I manage to free myself from my slacks. They fall, leaving me in my tented underwear.

Her eyes widen, and suddenly the fear that I saw in that guest bedroom is back. "What's wrong, Princess?" I ask, cupping her chin to stare in those nervous yet beautiful eyes.

"It's too damn big." I smirk, pride filling me.

"It will fit, and if not, I'll eat your pussy and finger fuck that tiny hole until your pretty cunt opens up enough to take my big dick, so relax." I drop my boxer briefs, and my dick proudly bobs against my stomach. It is massive, and I hate to admit it but I'm going to hurt her pussy the first time for sure.

Wrapping an arm around her waist, I move her onto the middle of the bed. I settle myself between her legs and kiss my way all over her body. I love the way she tastes, and I can't get enough of her. Natalya moans as I play with her massive breasts, teasing one with my hand while sucking on the other. Fuck, it's bliss.

I pop my lips off her tit and stare into her eyes. "I need to be inside you," I growl.

"Take me now and make me yours, Ilya." Rubbing the tip of my cock over her slit, I slide it along her folds, trying to maintain some control. I press the head inside and pleasure shoots through me, sending a spurt of cum along her opening. Fuck. Taking a deep breath, I push my way in until I'm fully buried inside her.

"Fuck, Princess. I'm so damn sorry."

"Don't be. I'm fine, Ilya. I promise. You're just so big," she grunts, pressing her hands to my chest, running them up over my shoulders. "I'll get used to you, so don't stop."

"Good, because I need to move." I rock my hips, rolling them into her. The tiny noises she makes go from grunts and yelps of pain to moans as her body begins adjusting to my size.

"Yes, Ilya. Just like that," she orders, thrusting her

pretty painted fingernails through my hair. A feral desire takes over, and I lose all sanity. My pace doubles and my body goes into overdrive as I fuck her pretty little hole until she's screaming my name for the third time.

Finally, I roar out hers, emptying my seed into her womb just like I planned. My mouth crashes down on hers, wanting this moment to last forever, but it can't, so I roll off my beautiful fiancée and drag her body onto mine so I can feel her heartbeat.

CHAPTER
EIGHT

NATALYA

OUR PASSION COMES TO AN END, but I didn't miss how many times his phone went off. I figure it had to do with my father, but then suddenly he jumps out of the bed in all his naked glory and hops in the shower. I look over at the clock and it's only eleven in the morning, so I lie down because my body is sore as hell. I just assume he's going to freshen up for round two or something, but when he comes out ten minutes later, he goes straight to his closet.

When he comes out, he's dressed in a pair of dark slacks and a sexy dark gray dress shirt, buttoned almost to the top. He puts his guns in place without saying anything to me, but his eyes are laser-focused on the mirror in front of him, looking right at me and my naked body that I haven't had the shame to cover.

"So damn sexy," he growls and shakes his head. "But you're missing something." He walks over and climbs onto the bed, straddling me. I don't miss how his cock is hard again and it's pinned right at my core, sending shivers through my body. Taking my hand in his, he slides a diamond ring onto my finger. "Perfect."

My mouth falls open as I stare at the massive six- to seven-carat stone on a platinum band. "Ilya…"

"What? This was supposed to be your present months ago."

"It's so big."

"Thanks," he says with a wink, grinding his hips into me.

"I meant the ring."

"Yes, that too." He kisses my lips until I'm breathless. Sliding away, he adds, "You deserve the best."

He gets off the bed, then steps back into his closet and slips on a suit jacket that matches his pants. Where is he going? What I deserve is for him to get naked and get back in bed with me.

"Be a good girl and stay put. It's extremely dangerous out there, and I'll be back soon."

"Where are you going?" I ask, sliding the cool sheets against my bare chest, suddenly feeling a bit embarrassed and naïve. This isn't how I expected the aftermath of losing my virginity to be. He was supposed to stay by my side and worship me until we both couldn't see straight and I couldn't move. Instead, he's eager to leave me.

"I have matters to deal with," he says as if it's the final answer I'll get from him. He comes back to the bed, kneeling on the mattress before he brushes his lips to my forehead. "Rest. I will be back soon."

He leaves me, and as soon as I hear the elevator close, I get up and use the bathroom. When I come out, I look around the bedroom, seeing a photo of me and him from my sweet sixteen on his nightstand that I hadn't noticed earlier. Smiling, I give it a kiss and then lie back down and take a nap.

I wake up and find out that I must have been exhausted because I slept almost four hours. Getting up, I slide on my panties and toss on one of his tee shirts. Thirsty, I pour myself a glass of water and admire his kitchen, which looks a lot like my mom's kitchen and reminds me of the time I begged him to kiss me. I miss Ilya.

When is he coming back? Then I remember my phone is tucked into the pocket of my dress. What if Ilya called me? I rush back into the bedroom and look for my clothes. Pulling it out, I turn it on and find a bunch of messages from my father, but none from Ilya. The last message is from my brother, and it sends me into a terrible place.

I play Junior's message back. *"Natalya, don't fall for his lies. I found out why he wasn't there for your birthday. He was shot while at a strip club by one of the whores that was blowing him. He was getting his dick sucked off on your birthday and got caught with his pants down."*

I try to call my brother back, but he doesn't answer.

Tears fall down my face. I need to get out of here before he comes back, but I don't know how much time I have. Quickly, I throw off his shirt, hating that just moments earlier I needed to be so close to him. His betrayal feels so unbelievably gut-wrenching the more I consider it.

Slipping on my clothes, I look around the apartment and find a piece of paper. I leave a note and set down the ring I only had the pleasure of wearing for just a few hours. There are only so many times that this man can break my heart. This is the final straw. There is no way to fix a shattered vessel.

My parents will understand when I return to their side. They love me unconditionally; this I am sure of. It may take time, but they'll help me make a life without Ilya and away from all things to do with our Russian side. I can't even imagine seeing him again or anyone who knows him.

Maybe my mother was right. I'm too young to understand relationships, and I need to date more before I find love. Ilya isn't the man I thought he was. My legs feel heavy as I move toward the exit, but my mind has been made up. There is no forgiving it.

Sneaking out onto the elevator, I take it down to the lobby, which is filled with several men in dark suits. Thankfully, none of them is Ilya. "Hey, you can't leave."

"Try to stop me and you'll be sorry." One tries to block the exit, but I kick the bastard in the balls. He crumbles to his knees, and although I should feel bad, right now is not the time. Looking down at him, I say, "You have your boss to thank for that."

Stepping around him, I walk right out the front door.

I send a message to my parents, hoping they can find me because I don't have any idea where I am.

I left Ilya. Please come and get me. I'm lost and have no idea where I am. I'll try to find somewhere to lay low.

Still, I leave my phone on and duck into one alleyway and then another. I don't know how long I will move about, but I don't want to be noticed by anyone related to the Semyonov family so that there's no danger to me.

My phone buzzes in my pocket with a message.

Stay put. I'm on my way.

Still, I decide to take a couple more turns. That's when I get an eerie feeling. It's a big mistake because in the next alley, there is a vehicle there waiting for me.

Suddenly a door swings open and a man comes for me, but I don't recognize him. "Ah, just the woman I'm looking for. You better be worth all the trouble you put me through, Amore. I will enjoy you many times before I return a piece to your father and then another piece to your lover." He's not Russian. I think he's Italian, but it doesn't make a difference because I'm full of fear.

I scream and run. I'm almost to the corner and onto the sidewalk when another vehicle comes up and the door flies open, and this time I'm grabbed roughly and thrown into the back with several men as the vehicle speeds off.

CHAPTER
NINE

ILYA

MY PHONE HAD BEEN RINGING off the hook while I was between Natalya's legs, worshiping my future. As much as I didn't want to leave her, I couldn't let the problem go unanswered.

Her father won't just let this go, and I don't want a war with the family I truly love. His betrayal came out of nowhere, and I can't understand why he'd let her move on when he knew I was in the midst of recovering and finding Fratelli. We had an understanding when it came to Natalya and he just stepped right over me. The more I think about it the angrier I become.

First, I must speak with my father before I do something crazy, like go to war with my godfather. It's the last thing I want to do, and yet the first thing that comes to mind.

As I prepared to leave, I remembered the last conversation Drago and I had about Natalya.

"It's not safe for Natalya with Fratelli roaming around."

"You have to deal with Fratelli sooner rather than later. Natalya and your future depends on it."

"Don't you think I know it?"

"Of course I do, Ilya, but you've already missed her birthday and you were almost killed."

"Exactly why it's not safe yet."

"Make it safe." He ends the call.

Before I head to the helipad, I address my men in one large group. "Keep an eye on my bride. Do not touch her; do not let her leave. If a hair is harmed on her head, it will be yours, understood?" My men knew my word was gold and Natalya was my everything. For the past year I'd been planning for her arrival until that bastard struck.

"Yes, sir," they chime in as a group.

I step onto the helipad and take the helicopter to our family's private landing strip, flying out right away because I need to see my father for his advice. I would bring Natalya with me, but the risk of bringing her out in the open with her parents' men as well as Fratelli out there is too dangerous. She's safe where they can't get to her.

It takes me four hours to get to my parents' and I second guess leaving Natalya every second that we're apart. Perhaps I should have let her visit continue because I never finished the deal for my father, and now he's going to be pissed about that. I shake my head and scratch that stupid thought. Hell if I was going to let Natalya be seduced by my best friend who has charm falling from his lips every single time a woman enters the room. He was on my side and wouldn't intentionally try to steal her, but he had a way about him.

"Where is Father?" I ask, entering the house in a hurry practically sprinting.

"In his office," my brother says. "Alone," he adds as I go down the hall in a mad dash. I forget that he and my mother could be completely occupied and that would force me to wait. Knocking rapidly, I don't wait for an answer. Storming in, I take a seat nearly tipping the leather chair backward.

His eyes widen like saucers with concern. "What's going on, son?"

"I crossed the line, but Drago crossed it first."

"What do you mean? Drago? Your godfather and my best friend?"

"Yes. I kidnapped Natalya." I jump out of my seat and pace in front of my father's desk, running my fingers through my hair.

He rubs his chin. "I heard they were coming soon, but I didn't realize they'd arrived already."

"Anatoly told me they were coming to meet with him, just her and Mrs. Romanov, as a potential suitor." I slam my hand on his desk.

"What?"

"Yes."

"Well, well." He thrusts his hands through his hair.

"This puts a riff in our friendship." That's an understatement.

"It does, but it doesn't change anything. Natalya is mine, and I made it so. He has called me, but I haven't answered it just yet because I wanted your advice."

He releases a harsh breath. "What are your plans with her?"

I thought that was obvious. The look of insanity on

my face. The risk of war with our closest family. "She's never leaving Russia again, unless we travel together as husband and wife."

"Well, then, I don't see a problem. I will speak with Drago, but damn it, you couldn't have just spoken to him?"

"I spoke with him before. I secured her safety, sent people to protect her, kept track of that stupid cunt while I hunted down our enemies, and this is how he repays me."

"Enough, Ilya. Please take caution. She's his baby girl, and daughters are precious. He loves you, but maybe he wanted to give her a chance to choose." I clamp my lips shut, my face heats with rage. The thought of her wanting anyone else causes my blood pressure to rise and my jaw to clench.

"She chose me, damn it."

"I will talk to him. Where is she?"

"In my bed, where she belongs."

"God, we need a wedding sooner rather than later."

"I'd have it tomorrow if I knew it was secure. Her safety is my priority."

"It can be done, but I'm sure your mother and hers wouldn't be pleased with a small wedding." I let out a chuckle and grin. It's the first time I've smiled since I left Natalya. Our mothers would skin me alive for rushing it.

"They better do it soon because I will not stop until she's carrying my sons."

"That's my boy." He winks and then stands up.

He chuckles and shakes his head before giving me a hug. "Careful—she has a lot of Rosalyn in her, and she'll give you shit."

"It's okay. I learned from her father, so it's his fault that I stole her in the first place." I chuckle, having learned how my godfather got my godmother.

My father's eyes fly open in shock that I dared to bring that up. "Don't tell him that." My father pours himself a drink.

"Contrary to my actions, I don't have a death wish," I say with a chuckle before leaving my father's office in a hurry.

I don't even bother greeting anyone else because I have to get back to my woman before it gets too late. It's still light out, but it won't be for very long. We board the plane and take off when my phone rings. It's my guards.

"She fled, Mr. Semyonov."

"What the fuck do you mean, she fled?" I bark out, rage, confusion, and pain striking me all at once. I shout toward the cockpit, "Fly faster." We have a private airport for a reason. I don't need anyone's permission to land as long as the airspace is clear, and it sure as fuck better be.

"She left after kicking Daniel in the balls." Why the fuck did she do that? I don't ask because my mind is reeling about the fact she's not in the condo where she's safe from danger, from Fratelli. Fucking Fratelli. In the back of my mind, I know he's behind this. That has to be the reason because she had no problem leaving her parents for me. Nothing would cause her to run away like that except him.

"And you let her leave," I snap, clenching my phone to the point I hear it crack, but rationality kicks in and I remember I need it.

"You said not to touch her."

Damn it. I did, but I never imagined she'd leave me after what we shared.

"Find her." I end the call, pacing the plane while I try to figure out my next steps.

It's everything she's wanted for the past several years, so why the hell would she leave? Where is she? I'm grateful that I was the one with access to track her phone, so that's what I do.

She's moving fast out of Omsk. Who is she with? Please tell me her asshole father got her.

A call comes in a second later, and it's Drago. "Where is she?" he asks me.

"Why the fuck would I tell you? So you could take her away from me?" I ask without any restraint left in me because he doesn't have her.

"You made my daughter run. Why would she flee from you and be ready to come back to us so soon? I trusted her with you." My mouth falls open from the sheer audacity.

"You trusted her with me? Don't talk about trust. You betrayed me and let Anatoly think he had a chance at her, and if he hadn't called me, then he'd have tried to seduce her," I bark out, hating the man I had spent all my life respecting as much as my own father.

"None of that matters. She's lost in a foreign city with God knows what kind of predators after her. Where is my daughter?" he says. He's right. All that matters is getting my love back.

"You're right. I'm tracking her now. She's headed toward one of my safe houses. Hold on, I have a call coming in from one of my men." I put the call on three-way so he can listen in.

"Boss, we have her. Sorry, but I had to grab her to get her in the vehicle. We didn't think it was safe to bring her back to the condo with Fratelli after her."

"Fratelli was after her?" Drago roars.

My guy pauses before continuing. "Yes, he nearly had her in the alley off Capitol Café. We spotted her and scooped her up. She tried to fight me, but I swear, I only tried to get her in the vehicle and lock her in before Fratelli opened fire." That fucking bastard shot at my woman. I swallow the lump in my throat before I can speak again.

"No, you did good. We're on our way. Keep her safe, even from herself. Don't let her escape again," I say, knowing what that means.

"Are you sure?" The hesitation and fear in his voice isn't just because I'll kill him if he fucks up, but because Natalya's a damn tiger and she's going to put up a fight.

"Yes—but be gentle," I add.

"She's rough," he answers, sounding just as afraid of Natalya as he is me. I can hear Drago chuckling on the other end.

"She's my queen and Drago Romanov's daughter. Expect no less."

I end the call with both of them intentionally. It's childish, but he dared flaunt my woman in front of other men as if they had a chance and that burns deep in my gut.

He calls back a minute later. "Are you done with your tantrum?"

"Signal lost. I'm on a plane, after all. Would you like the location of the safe house?"

"I'm surprised you'd even consider letting me in."

"Letting you?" I scoff because this fucker could storm in if he wanted. He's only gotten sharper with age.

"Send the coordinates and we'll talk later."

"Will do." I end the call and wait five minutes before sending the location. He'll be a few minutes behind me, so I'll have some time with my wily bride-to-be.

CHAPTER
TEN

ILYA

IT TAKES another half hour for my pilot and I to get into the helicopter. Soon we're up in the air, and shortly we land on the property where my guards are waiting with my little devil-queen, bound up.

Ivan stands outside, watching the perimeter nearby with a scowl and his hand bandaged. I nod and then continue to the entrance. Piotr stands outside the door and says, "She bit him."

"Oh. Damn. I better stand at a good distance."

"I would if I was you, boss." He opens the door and there she is bound to a chair in the middle of the room, looking feisty and gorgeous as ever. There aren't any marks on my woman except probably where she's actively trying to free herself from her ropes.

"Well, hello, princess."

Her head lifts and her eyes meet mine with fire in those stunning blues. "You," she hisses, attempting to tug herself free. "You did this to me."

"I didn't do this to you. You did this to yourself. If you'd just kept your pretty ass in bed like the dutiful wife you're supposed to be, then you'd be perfectly fine. Now your father's on his way, and he and I are going to have to straighten your ass out."

"What? Me? You have some motherfucking audacity."

"Princess, I like your filthy mouth in bed, but here, it's not so nice." I wag my finger at her but not so close to her pretty, fierce mouth.

"You betrayed me, and you think I give a fuck what you like or care to be nice," she says, spitting at my feet in pure disgust.

"Leave us," I bark out to my men. I still refuse to let my little snow tiger go free because she's going to unleash those claws and I'm her kill.

I walk up to her, press my hand on the back of her chair, lean down, and stare into her gorgeous eyes. "Now, do you care to explain how I betrayed us?"

"You were at a strip club on my birthday getting your dick hard, and that's why you ended up shot." Behind the venom in her words are the unshed tears in her eyes.

I grab her face, pinching her cheeks. "Watch your mouth, little girl, because those lies are going to get you punished." Letting go, I take a step back and run my hands through my hair.

"First off, I wasn't at the strip club on your birthday; it was a few days before, and it wasn't to get horny. Thinking about you does a good job of stiffening my dick,

I admitted just as the door opened.

"Whoa. Hold the fuck up. Don't make me kill you." Fuck. I should have told them not to let Drago in until I was prepared, but then again, he might have come in guns blazing.

"Godfather," I say, feeling the slightest bit of embarrassment and a hint of fear. This man taught me how to kill and how to do it well.

"Daddy," Natalya calls out like a sweet little innocent princess instead of the little pit viper who was just spitting venom and biting.

"Why is she still tied up?" he asks, glaring at me and ready to untie his little girl.

"Because she hasn't learned to behave yet."

"Fuck off, you piece of shit." She jerks in her chair, hissing at me, trying to kick me but the guys tied her ankles. There goes her true colors.

Her father nods his head, crosses his arms, and says, "Fair enough." Damn that burns. I've been his loyal dog for years, protecting his family, especially Natalya while he double crossed me.

"What? You're sticking up for him when you didn't even want me to marry him?"

He shakes his head, pulls a chair close to Natalya, and takes a seat. "I never said that, my dear girl. I don't want you to be married to anyone yet, but if there is anyone, it's Ilya."

She tilts her head and stares at him in complete confusion. "Then why did you say he was marrying someone in a Russian family within the next year?"

He clamps his mouth shut and breathes through his nose, rubbing his hands on his thighs before saying, "Are we not a Russian family?"

"Are you kidding me?" Now her temper has turned on him. I cross my arms and smirk.

He looks at both of us and says, "I expected your mothers to take months to plan a wedding." Then he crunches his knuckles and continues, "I had other reasons. Even after vetting your friends, I didn't trust them."

"But you knew how devastated I was, and you could have told me." Fuck. Her voice cracking almost sends me to my knees. The thought of her heart breaking for no damn reason guts me. I've loved her for so long. She has no need to feel pain except for missing me.

"I could have said something, yet every time I asked you how you felt about Ilya, you lied to me." She has the shame to duck her head and blush. I love the pretty pink that dusts her cheeks.

I tip her chin and say, "You look down to no one."

"Are you going to untie me?" she questions, looking at me with sad eyes, but I'm still not sure if she's going to leave me, and I can't let that happen. I love this woman to the point of madness. There's no way in hell I'll let her go.

"Not until you tell me why you ran off, and where the fuck is your diamond ring?"

"It's at the condo. I got a voicemail from Junior who told me you were at the club when you were shot. I felt hurt and lied to. I was kept caged while you did whatever you pleased."

"Your brother said that?" I could snap his fucking neck. We didn't get along for so long. I wonder if he just played nice this past year as an act.

"Yes."

"No, he didn't," my godfather says, shaking his head.

"I have the voicemail," Natalya insists, so I open my phone and log into her phone, checking her messages and finding the one that supposedly came from her brother, but the number comes up spoofed and it's not his. I play it on speaker, getting pissed off by the second. "What the fuck? You have access to my phone."

"I told you; you were mine, and I'd do anything to protect you."

Drago shakes his head. "Your brother is on a special... mission and isn't available for the next two days. He has no idea that you're here or even that we were looking for you." I knew there was something up with the spoofed number.

"What?"

"It could be AI-generated," I explain, reaching around and untying my future wife.

Her hand comes out and slaps me across the face. "What the fuck were you doing in a strip club in the first place?" I suppose I had that one coming.

"Anatoly needed help finding some of his girls that were kidnapped, and the kidnapper requested that a ransom be delivered by me. I was in his office—not watching the entertainment—when we had our meeting. We were headed out the back entrance when we were both shot, along with some of our men." She gasps, her mouth falling open. My hands go to her legs, and I cut the ties on her ankles. I remember her hand running over the scar, and I didn't let her ask the question.

"Did you get the girls back?" I rub her wrists, placing kisses on her sore and reddened flesh.

I shake my head. "No, the bastard had no intention of giving them back. He killed them well before requesting the money. It was a game for the sick Italian fuck."

She gasps and then says, "There was an Italian who

found me when I left the condo, and he said he was looking for me."

"He probably was waiting for the perfect moment to strike," Drago mutters.

"Who is he?" she asks, looking back and forth between us.

"Nico Fratelli."

Natalya starts. "I've heard that name before." I've never shared that information. I look at Drago to see what he's revealed. He shakes his head.

"What do you mean?" her father asks. He keeps his business away from his family, except for Junior, of course, who is following in his footsteps.

"Rachel was dating a guy named Nico recently, and then I remember her asking me if I wanted to meet up at their family restaurant, Fratelli's, but I told her I couldn't because we were leaving for Russia."

"Rachel?" Drago asks. He knows all of her friends and did background checks on them before allowing them back into her life.

"Yes."

"Fuck, are all your friends shady?" I ask, hating all those bitches and wanting to cut them all from her life. It will help that we're going to be thousands of miles and continents apart.

"Rachel's not like that." She's shaking, and her eyes are filled with tears again. Damn it, I don't like that shit one bit, so I pull her into my arms.

"Maybe he got to her and charmed his way into her life," Drago says.

"It's possible. The bastard is going to pay." My fists clench behind Natalya's back as I hold her close.

"Where is Mom?" she asks.

"She's with Roman and Katya. I thought it was safer for them to keep an eye on the rest of my family."

I turn to Drago and shake my head because he's got a lot to answer for, even if he's pissed at me. "It is, which is why I don't understand why you brought Natalya here. I told you I'd come when I had things wrapped up."

"Ilya, you were running ragged trying to find that fucker. Day and night, no fucking rest while you weren't even healed, and my daughter sat at home, miserable. Like you said, you're the best person to protect her. You literally stole her right in front of my wife and dared my wrath. No man would challenge me for her hand, and trust me, I've had offers, but I already gave you my blessing. I'm sorry that I made you think otherwise."

"Offers? Who?" I challenge. I'll fucking slit their throats.

"Not important."

"The hell it isn't."

"I'm curious," Natalya says, testing my patience in front of her father. She doesn't realize that I'm on the verge of losing my mind already. I nearly lost her today, and the only thing keeping me off her is the fact that her father is feet from us with a loaded weapon. I'd pin her to the wall and stuff her with my cock or tie her back up and fuck her roughly until she understands what she means to me.

"You better get uncurious, Princess."

There's a rapid knock on the front door. "What's going on?" I call out, pushing Natalya behind me.

"We have a fix on Fratelli." It's Piotr, so I open the door for my team and then my guard continues. "We triangulated all the cameras. In his rush to get your fiancée, he messed up and let his cover slip."

I meet with my men outside where they've stationed a tracking system and learn what they have on Fratelli's whereabouts. My lead technician has been tracking his movements through Omsk, and he's headed toward my hideout. The only way he'd know where she was is if he has her phone location pinged. He's not far out anymore.

"I have a plan," I say. "We need to move, so pack it up," I tell them. Heading inside, I pull Natalya to my side and kiss her temple. "He's on his way here, but I have a plan to finally get rid of that fuck."

"Go ahead," Drago says.

I lay it out, but Natalya's not happy with the risks. She's looking at her father with tears and guilt in her eyes.

My godfather pulls her into his arms and says, "It's fine, sweetling. I'm looking forward to greeting this bastard. I trust Ilya not to miss his target."

"You know I won't." It's a promise I can easily make because I'm an expert shot even at a distance while chasing a moving target.

I checked the time and distance from Nico's position and ours. We're about twenty minutes from his location, so we head out, moving in modes of transportation.

I have Natalya with me in the helicopter while her father rides with her phone in the vehicle on the back roads that lead back to Omsk. It's not long before a black SUV races down the same road at a high rate of speed. We know it has to be him because of the trace, and sure as fuck no one else is traveling down this hidden path.

Suddenly Fratelli makes Drago's SUV and speeds up behind him at over a hundred miles an hour.

Using my heat-signature weapon, I scan his black SUV and I look through it, spotting him with the driver.

Drago slows down, attempting to act as if he's going to move over and let the driver pass, so Fratelli slows and moves behind him. They're both traveling at forty miles an hour when Fratelli speeds up, tailing behind Drago's vehicle, ready to hit the bumper and send it into a ditch, but we're prepared. I take my sniper shot, hitting his tire and sending Fratelli's vehicle spinning, and then I shoot the engine with several rounds. It comes to a screeching halt, almost teetering off into a ditch.

Four minutes later, I get a call from my future father-in-law. "Son, I have a present I'd like to share with you. How about we have a family dinner at your parents' tomorrow and then we can celebrate?" We're closer to Omsk than St. Petersburg so Drago has a long way, but he's going to take my parents' private plane with our guest while we take the helicopter home.

"Yes, I'd like that. Should I invite Petrov?" I ask.

"Yes. As I recall, he'd love to crack open this gift."

"Sounds good." We end the call, and I fly my princess back to the condo because there's something I need to do before we can join my family at the estate tomorrow and we have time to spare.

CHAPTER
ELEVEN

NATALYA

WE ENTER the condo in complete silence and my body's filled with tension, anticipating his anger. He hasn't said a word since we exited the helicopter on the roof.

He empties his pockets, setting his keys and wallet into a bowl by the door. Then he slides off his suit jacket, revealing his shoulder holsters and massive guns that frame sides. Damn, he looks intimidating and yet my body is burning with lust. "How are your wrists?"

I look at the redness and rub the sore spots. "They're sore, but they'll be fine soon."

He let out a curt, "Good." I barely draw my gaze up toward him when he throws me over his shoulder and carries me to the sofa. With a swift twist and turn, I'm lying on my stomach over his knees. The cool breeze of my dress flipping over my back and my panties swiftly sliding down my legs shocks me.

"What the hell?" I say, trying to scramble away.

"Did you think that stunt you pulled would go unpunished?" he questions. There's a heated tone in his voice that sends my pulse racing with desire.

I turn my head to him, lifting one hand so he can see my wrist. "Tying me to a chair wasn't punishment enough?" I remind him.

He snarls and pops my ass with a hard smack. The sting burns on my soft skin, but then his rough hands massage the heated flesh. "Thank you for reminding me. This is for the chair. You forced my guards to put their hands on you. Do you think I want another man to touch your beautiful skin? You belong to me. You're my queen, and no one touches you but me. They did it to save your life at the risk of my wrath."

That's why they let me leave so easily, and I'm the fool for running. I ran straight into the hands of the devil. If they didn't come for me, I would have been brutally violated and then dead. "I'm sorry."

"It's too late for sorry, little girl. You're going to take your punishment like a good girl, and then you're going to ride my cock." I nod. He gives me another spank on my other cheek before roughly massaging the reddened spot, and although it stings and tears flood my ducts, another part of me begins to soak. Holy hell. My thighs slam together.

"No. Don't close up on me, Princess." He roughly tugs my thighs apart. Another strike comes down, and this time it's right on my pussy. I swear I'm on the verge of coming. How is that possible? Squirming against his strong thighs, I hold on as he continues my punishment, delivering a few more blows to my ass, massaging my round cheeks after each spanking.

"So red. My fucking favorite color," he growls. "Time to see how much you enjoyed your punishment." He stuffs his meaty finger into my pussy and I clench around it, soaking his digit with how horny I am.

"Ilya," I moan, pussy fluttering on the edge of an orgasm.

"So ready." He lifts me off his thick, muscular legs and flips me so my stomach hits the back of the sofa and my knees are on the cushions. "Hold on because I'm not going to be so fucking nice to you. You scared me today; you scared your father today. You put yourself in danger, and I need to feel you." I hear the metal from his belt clang as he takes it off and then his zipper before he pulls my hips further back and pushes my head down.

The blunt tip of his cock rubs against my soft entrance, and I nearly scream out as he hesitates. "Forever mine." With one hand on my hip, he pushes his way into my body, sending his cock deep inside me. My breath catches from the fullness, and I can hardly see straight. He wraps his muscular arms around my chest, bear hugging me as his mouth nuzzles my throat, clinging to me while pumping into my tiny hole. The pleasure of his grip on me is intense, and my orgasm is immediate. I cry out in his arms, unable to hold back.

"That's it. Let me hear it. I love you, Natalya."

"I love you, Ilya." His strong hand grips my face, turning it and then his mouth is on mine, kissing me deeply as his last deep stroke fills me with his seed. We don't stop kissing until he finishes emptying inside of me.

"Now my son is inside of you."

"I hope so," I whisper against his lips. He pulls out of me and then lifts me up, carrying me to the bathroom. He hits the light switch and then sets me on the toilet while he moves to his large shower stall, turning it on.

"We must shower, eat, and rest. Tomorrow, we go to see your parents."

"Aren't we going to see yours?" I thought we were going to St. Petersburg.

"Yes, but I care not if my parents know if you're covered in my scent. I don't believe your father will appreciate it until you're my wife." He smirks at me like he knows how much trouble he's in and loving it.

"I don't believe he'll ever appreciate it."

"True, but I don't care." I knew it. He actually enjoys goading my father. "You're mine and he knows it, so he'll have to get used to it once we're married. You're going to be carrying my children and they aren't going to appear out of thin air."

He kisses me roughly and helps me into the shower. "Where are you going?"

"To use the other shower because there is no way I'm showering with you and keeping my hands to myself."

"Okay." I wash up, noticing the unopened bottles of my favorite shampoos, which they don't have here in Russia. The man had prepared for my arrival. How could I ever doubt his love for me? Once I'm done, I wrap myself in his fluffy towels and head into his bedroom. There's just one problem: my clothes, especially my panties, aren't fit to wear back to his parents' today.

"Damn, Princess, you look so delectable." I stare at him with his towel wrapped just around his waist, water glistening on his broad chest, the smattering of hair darkened by the wetness. I want to run my hands over him. "Stop looking at me like that. I need to feed you and when you look at me like that, the only thing I want to stuff down your throat is my big cock."

"Well, that can be for dessert," I tease, giving him a wink. "Also, I might remind you I don't have any clothes except the ones I wore here."

He scoffs. "Come, my lovely bride." He takes my hand and opens the door leading to his insanely large closet that makes my mother's closet look small. She's seriously going to lose her mind when she sees this. "This is your section here. I had these brought in over the past couple of months."

My eyes nearly pop out of my head and my mouth falls open. "Are you serious?" I don't think I've ever seen a closet so large.

"Why not? I figured you would need a lot of clothes as my wife. Now, you'll have a pretty dress and shoes for tomorrow. Some undergarments, I suppose. My mother and sister did all the shopping for me, so I would be surprised if there aren't any. I hope it's to your liking."

"It is, Ilya. It's perfect."

"It's missing one thing." He takes my hand and slides my ring onto my finger. "Perfect. Don't ever take it off again."

"I won't." I stand on my tiptoes and kiss his scruffy chin.

"Let's get some food inside both of us because we need it. If you keep it up, I'm going to fuck you all over again. Look at what you did. I'm already getting hard, and we both need our strength." I stare down at his massive cock and groan. It's so perfect, and I lick my lips.

"No, you will have to wait. Food first." He wags his finger at me, and I nod.

"Yes, my future husband." He carries me to bed and finds his shirt there. "I was wearing that earlier."

"Put it back on," he growls. He flips it the right way and hands it to me. I slip it on, and I watch as his eyes darken, lust filling them.

"Uh-oh," I squeal, jumping on the bed. He pounces on me, and our meal has to wait a little longer.

I WAKE UP, AND ILYA HAS BEEN BUSY THIS MORNING BECAUSE the bed is cold, which pisses me off. I climb out of it and find him in his office working on documents. It's then I remember that he's actually a busy man. Since I fell in love with him, my plans have revolved around being his wife and nothing more. Never once had I considered what I wanted to be other than Mrs. Ilya Semyonov. As his wife, I didn't need to do a damn thing, and he wouldn't want me to have a career because the risk to my safety would be too intense.

"Do you need any help?" I ask as if I know what to do.

"I could really use some assistance."

"Oh yeah?" I answer.

"Yes, here. My lips are terribly lonely." Smiling, I walk over around his desk and plant myself in his lap before kissing his lips.

When I step back, I bat my eyelashes and ask, "Did I do a good job?"

"Fabulous, but I'm going to need that job done on a permanent basis."

"I believe I'm up to the task." I could kiss this man all day long and never get bored.

He rubs my back and tugs at the bottom of my long hair. "So are you hungry?"

"A little."

"My chef will make us some food shortly."

"You have a chef?" We hadn't met anyone last night and we'd made our own dinner, which was simple wrapped-up food that I thought his mother had brought over.

"Not often, but since I knew you'd be here, I made sure that she'll be here at your request."

An instant flare of jealousy shoots through my body. "She?"

"She's older than my mother, and totally not my type."

"Not your type?" Who the hell is his type other than me? I've lost my appetite and am about to just skip out on breakfast.

"Nope. Not a bratty little Russian-American with trust issues and an exquisite body that has my heart, body, soul."

"Fair enough. I'm pretty sure that's a rare breed."

"Extremely rare. Only one of a kind. Now, let's get some clothes on you before it's too late and I have to stab someone's eyeballs out of their sockets."

"Oh, yummy, makes me so hungry," I grumble, rolling my eyes. "Besides, she's a woman. I doubt she cares."

"It's that wonderful bratty attitude I love so much, and I care." I get dressed, and we head into the kitchen where there is a sweet older woman cooking. "Princess, this is my chef, Olga. Olga, this is my lovely Natalya."

She says something in Russian that I don't

understand, but Ilya quickly translates. "She said you are more beautiful than your pictures." I blush.

"Thank you," I say in Russian. It's one of the few words I've learned over the years. My father's distaste for his roots hadn't quite changed over the years, so although he spoke the language, he didn't force us to learn. My older brothers know it well and I should have learned it, but I'm not the brightest student.

"Sit. I make food."

"Olga is learning English so that she can take care of your needs when I'm not around." I look up at my future husband and press my palm on his chest with a smile.

"That's so sweet." Olga smiles politely as she makes us some food. Ilya speaks to her in Russian and then she slowly speaks to me in broken English before going back to the stove. Ilya sees her out because we won't be home for a few days, while I pack a bag to take to his parents. My body anticipates his entrance before he enters the room. Pulse racing, heart pounding, pussy throbbing with need. I love this man so much.

He comes up behind me and slides his hands under my top, wrapping them around my waist. "So perfect."

"We should be leaving," I remind him.

"Yes, we should," he answers with his lips on my ear, taking the tiniest nibble.

"Ilya," I moan, sliding my hands down his thighs. "Perhaps we have some time."

"Yes, we do." He pulls down my shorts and panties. "Bend over, baby." He pushes my back and I press my palms flat on the comforter. He swiftly frees himself and then his round head rubs up and down along my slit, sliding into my slick entrance.

"Oh, Ilya." His hands cup my tits, squeezing them as he leans over my back and pumping into me so deep, I'm gasping for air.

"Damn that's so sexy. Those sounds coming from your throat. Come for me, my princess. Come for me."

"Oh, God, I am." I clench up, fisting the sheets and shout his name as my thighs shake.

"Good girl," he roars, filling me up with each thrust until he gives me every last drop. Our clothes are wrinkled and bunched up, covered in sweat when we finally pull apart.

"Oh, no. I'm a sticky, sweaty mess again," I say with a smirk. "I have to go wash up."

"Okay, but don't take too long. We have to leave soon."

"Yes, Mr. Semyonov." I salute him and scurry into the bathroom with his seed dripping down my inner thighs. Although I attempt to take a fast shower, I start thinking about us and lose myself in thought until I realize I've been in there for half an hour. Finally, I turn off the water and come out wrapped in a big fuzzy towel.

Several expletives leave his mouth when I come out of the bathroom. "What's wrong?"

Quickly he crosses the distance, wraps his hand around the back of my neck, and pulls me in for a kiss that steals my breath. "Enough. Dress now, or we won't make it at all." He grunts and withdraws, taking my towel with him and bringing it to his nose. "I always loved your scent, my menace."

He doesn't look back at me as he slides into the bathroom, turning on the shower again. Ignoring him, I dive into the amazing closet and find the cutest dress with a matching bra and panty set. When I'm finally fit to be his adoring fiancée, I step out and look for a brush because my long hair needs to be tamed.

A minute later, Ilya comes out and says, "Well, that was a waste."

"You don't like my outfit?"

"I meant the cold shower." Giggling, I duck my head into my chest and shake my head. He kisses the crown of my head and says, "What happened to your necklace?"

I blush and duck my head in shame. "I was hurt when my father said you were getting married, and I..."

He tips my chin up so that he gets a full view of my eyes. "You what?"

"I threw them away."

"Oh." He smiles to himself. "Well, my beloved, I will just have to replace them."

"I'm sorry."

"Don't be sorry, unless you're lying."

"I'm not. I wish I didn't because it was my favorite piece, and I never took it off except when it was lost in the pool." He frowns again, and then he's on his phone.

"Don't cry. I never want to see your tears unless they're for pleasure." He takes the brush from my hand and slides it through my thick, long hair. "One day, I want a little princess just like you."

"One day."

We finally leave his condo, and I'm nervous the entire helicopter flight because we have to face my father and we never got past the whole relationship issue. My almost-abduction was a bigger issue than Ilya's actions. Now that Fratelli isn't a problem, I wonder how my father will handle it.

As the helicopter lands and the blades stop twirling,

the entire Semyonov family gathers outside with my parents. A bottle of champagne is popped, and a bunch of confetti is released. "Congratulations, Ilya and Natalya," they cheer.

"My baby girl," my mother says, running to meet us halfway. She throws her arms around me. "I was so worried."

"But you saw him take me." My head tilts, wondering why she's acting like she didn't know he was taking me when she practically shoved me into his arms.

"I'm not talking about Ilya."

"Oh, you knew?"

"Yes. I was with your father, and then he sent me with some of Petrov's men to be protected. We were immediately brought here."

"I'm so sorry."

"Don't be sorry." She hugs me tightly. "Your father explained it all to me. I would be upset as well."

My father is next, pulling me into his arms. "My little bird, are you well?"

"Yes, Father. I'm sorry I caused you so much trouble."

"You did nothing but take a few years off my life. I suppose it is good that you're marrying young, then. Are you angry with Ilya?"

"No. I knew what I did would force him to act." He kisses my temple and leads me toward my future in-laws.

"Come here, sweet Natalya." Mrs. Semyonov pulls me in and hugs me tightly. "I'm so happy that you're going to be my daughter as well. Although, it feels like you've always been."

"Thank you. I'm thrilled as well."

"You all took a long time to get here," my father says to Ilya.

"We had to discuss some matters, and I had to show my new bride one of her future homes." My father cocks his brow, eyeing Ilya with a death glare.

"Mom, you should see the closet. It's insane. You're going to want Daddy to have one built for you."

"Oh, at the condo?" Ilya's mother says. "It's exquisite. Ilya wanted you to have the best."

"I love it."

"I will have to see it, but we have so much to discuss before the wedding."

"Speaking of weddings, when will that work for you?" Ilya asks me.

"Two months ago, but I'll be happy when it comes."

"We are ready to have it in the next week."

"Good." He kisses my hand and leads us into the house.

CHAPTER
TWELVE

ILYA

"MAY I have a word with you in private?" Drago asks. I am already prepared for the onslaught that I'm about to receive.

"You can use my office," my father says. We stand and exit the room before Natalya can stop me. She's anxious, but Drago isn't going to misbehave in front of my parents, even if he's pissed off with me. We enter the room, and I close the door. He pulls me into his arms and gives me a hug. "I'm so glad you're alive." I'm shocked by his reaction, but as we break apart, he says, "When your father called me to tell me what happened at the club, I prayed that you survived not only for Natalya's sake, but for my own. You're my godson, and although you're stealing my little girl, you know that I've always thought of you as another son."

"Thank you. I hadn't expected you to care after..."

"After you essentially kidnapped my daughter?"

"Yes."

"My wife and I were well aware of what we were doing. As I said before, she was safer and happier with you. The Fratelli family have agents ready to strike at home as well. As you see, they were ready to snatch her up if she'd gone out with one of her friends."

"True."

"Now, I'm sure they're worried I'm tearing into you in here, and although I've let you off easy, I will give you a warning. You hurt my baby girl, and I'll forget all the love I have for you."

"You know that I wouldn't harm her."

"Except the ropes earlier."

"Actually, the ropes were for her own safety. You saw that she was trying to escape again."

"Fair enough."

"Where is her necklace? She told me she threw it away." I eye him because the damn thing has been tracked to the house. He opens his jacket, and he pulls out the little box.

"I knew she treasured it," he confesses, having pulled it from the trash.

"Give it to her as a wedding present."

"Don't you want to give it back to her?"

"No. You rescued it from the trash, and she'll be happy to have it back." We shake hands and then embrace. "Thank you, Godfather." We leave my father's office and return to the family with smiles on our faces.

Natalya's eyes meet mine, and she blushes. "Sorry I'm late, but I had another matter to see to," Anatoly says, coming from the other entrance of the dining room.

"Welcome. You're just in time to celebrate the engagement."

"Congratulations, Ilya and Ms. Natalya. You are with the better man." He winks at her, and I still want to punch him in the head or balls but I let it go for the time being because I want to kiss my bride.

I lean down and steal a chaste kiss from Natalya's lips, or at least attempt to do so because she lets out a seductive moan in front of our entire family. I groan and pull back, taking my seat beside my fiancée.

"I'm glad it's only a week away because they can't keep their hands off each other," Natalya's sister says.

"Young love."

"Please," my brother scoffs.

"What's that supposed to mean, young man?" my father asks.

"We all know to keep our distance from a closed door when you and Mother are inside."

"It's the same in our house as well. Young love—yeah, right," Natalya says. "I only hope to have a love like that in thirty years."

"We will." I raise her hand to my lips and kiss the back of it. "I promise."

After dinner, coffee and vodka are brought around, and we talk of wedding plans. However, there is another matter on my mind—one that won't go away until I'm sure it's dead and buried. My fingers itch, rubbing the rim of my cold glass as I sit making small talk.

"Men, I believe the wedding talk should be left for the ladies. We have some things to handle," my father says. There is a look shared between the men and a smile stretches across my face. I've been waiting for this moment, itching to take my revenge and when I look at my godfather, his expression mirrors mine. Although, the fucker is definitely more menacing. We stand and say a brief goodbye to each of our women before leaving the table.

"Yes, please do handle it soon because it will take a long time," my godmother, Rosalyn, says with a viciousness I've only heard about and yet never witnessed. That is exactly where Natalya gets that strength from, and I know that one day she'll rule strongly beside me.

My little queen pushes her chair back and walks around to where us men have congregated toward the dining room door. "Before you go, I want to tell you what Fratelli said to me."

"Go on," her father says, teeth clenched, tension radiating off him. I know anything Fratelli said would be brutal and fucked up, but I hold back my rage.

"He said that after he was done using me, he was going to send a piece of me to my father, and then another piece of me to my lover." I could almost hear my teeth crack when she finished.

"My beloved, thank you for telling us. Now, go on and plan our wedding." I kiss her temple, and her father kisses her forehead. "Let's send a piece to his family and his men." I crack my knuckles.

"Damn right. The bastard dared to threaten my baby." Drago pulls out a blade from his pocket, opening it up and brushing it against his chin. "I'm going to enjoy every minute of this."

"Remember, men. We have to make this last," my father says.

Drago claps my father's shoulder, nodding. "Yes, Roman. I want him to slowly die. Every single one of us has a need to exact revenge on this piece of shit." My father wants to make him pay for hurting me and scaring my parents. My near death sent them into a terrible place, and they want Fratelli to pay for his crimes.

We open the room where our special guest is waiting, and he's nearly pissing in his pants but the bravado hasn't left him yet. "So, it takes all of you to come after me because he's too weak to face me alone?" he asks, pointing his insult at me.

"No. Your death has been earned by the hand of each and every one of us. Unfortunately, we can't decide who should get the kill, so we'll all take turns destroying you until all that's left are the pieces we send to your family."

"Wait—maybe we can work something out."

"There's nothing to work out. You tried to kill my son on more than one occasion." My father takes the first strike, sending Nico flailing back on the floor, chains clanging. He attempts to throw an arm up to block the next strike, but my father has a practiced fist and switches his swing to a side buster.

Anatoly steps up. He grips Fratelli by his black and gray hair, yanking it back, and pulls out his own blade. "You killed my innocent employees, you almost killed me, and you tried to kill my oldest friend." With a painfully slow slice, he scalps a generous chunk from Fratelli's head. Damn, Petrov's sicker than I thought.

Stepping back, it's my godfather's turn. "You tried to kidnap my daughter five times. The people you sent in to take my princess failed every time because we love her with everything we have. You picked the wrong families to fuck with." I look at him strangely because I only know of the three times.

"I didn't give you the tip for the warehouse for no reason. He came for her before her sweet sixteen. I thought that would be a lesson to him. Hell, I even let him know that was for trying to nab my daughter, but he didn't learn." He takes his blade and goes to town, slicing cuts as Fratelli tries to shield himself but it does no good.

My godfather reins in his violence and steps back. He turns to me, wiping the blood off his cheek. "I'm not done, but I don't want him to pass out before you get your turn." The demon is in his eyes, and I nod.

Smiling at the stupid fucking pussy, I consider how I'll destroy him, but he's barely hanging on. "This is all over wanting my woman."

"She would have made a perfect whore for the market or my bed," he spits out. We know he deals in human trafficking, but the words are enough for all of us.

"You couldn't just leave well enough alone. No, you just couldn't."

The violent rage in me is too intense, but I know that once I start, I won't stop. "Now—I don't have enough restraint to stop from killing you." I step back and look at my godfather. "Drago, I offer you this gift for giving me Natalya's hand."

He smiles. "Are you sure?"

"Yes. I will kill him if I touch him, and you won't get another chance. As her father, I think you deserve it. Besides, I won't make it slow." The thought of him touching my little Natalya or selling her to some sick fuck is too much. I want to smash his head into the ground.

Drago takes his time, and we watch as he drags out the torture, painstakingly drawing out Nico Fratelli's death until there isn't a breath left in his body.

"Thank you, my boy," he says.

"Thank you for keeping her safe before I knew she was in danger."

"That's why I put a tracker in her pendant the first time."

"Oh." I wondered why he'd done that since she was always with her guards and had her phone on her at all times.

"Just in case she was taken. She never took it off, and it was such a small trinket, they wouldn't think it was valuable enough to be worth money, or so I thought."

"The guy stole it probably for proof that he had his hands on her, or just got lucky and ran off with it. He had an addiction and wanted to pawn it."

"True."

"Hey, let's get this mess cleaned up and get back to our families."

"Yes, I have someone waiting for me." Anatoly gives me a wink. I shake my head because the man will never settle down. The time it takes to deal with the piece of filth and clean up put us well past midnight, and our families have all gone to bed.

I wonder where my mother set up Natalya for the evening. Would they keep us apart because her parents are here and we aren't married, or would they understand how much we need each other?

I open my bedroom door, and my beautiful fiancée is lying on my bed like the dirty fantasy I had too many times. She's in just a tee shirt of mine, which has risen up, revealing a pair of black panties that I want to tear off her. The anger and rage I never got to unleash sends adrenaline and hunger through my veins.

NATALYA

THE WOMEN and my younger sister don't seem bothered by the fact that the guys have been gone so long. The rest of my siblings keep busy in the gaming room while the men are dealing with my would-be kidnapper. I try to focus on the bridal stuff, but all I want to do is go to bed and wait for Ilya to join me.

I let out a yawn, which caught my mother-in-law's eye. "I'm sorry, you have to be exhausted after everything. We can call it a night and focus on more tomorrow."

"Thank you so much. It's been such an emotional and trying couple of days, and I'm really tired."

"You need rest. Plus, I'm sure Ilya's going to be worried if you're still up when they're done."

"He said for us to continue planning."

"Yes, but it will be a while, so we put you in Ilya's room." She smiles, and my mom pretends to pay no mind to it. I'm sure they left that part out to my father; at least he didn't bother to ask. He wasn't too pleased that we arrived pretty late today and knew what we must have been up to last night and this morning. Even if we were married, I wouldn't expect him to feel comfortable with us sharing a bedroom. I'm still his little girl.

When I go up to his bedroom, I close the door and breathe in. It's so him, even though he doesn't really stay here. The first thing I notice, besides the cleanliness, is my picture on his wall and on his nightstand. I wonder how long he's had these pictures up, and does everyone know about them?

Feeling sleepy, I undress down to my panties and then dig through one of his drawers and pull out a shirt, sliding it over my head. I have only just closed my eyes when the door opens and my handsome, dangerous fiancé enters the room with a feral look in his eyes. I know he has to have me, and I slide my legs open, welcoming him.

WAKING UP IN HIS ARMS, MY BODY HAS NEVER FELT SO protected, safe, content. I'm so glad he fell in love with me the way I'm in love with him. All these years, Ilya has cared for me. Of course, I'm not sure when he finally decided it was more than innocent. Was it the party last year?

"Good morning, Princess." I roll over and see that he's staring right into my eyes.

"Good morning. How long have you been awake?"

"A while. Tell me what's on your mind." I pause before considering what to say. "Don't hold back, my love.

I want you to tell me what you're thinking. Are you bothered about what we did last night?"

"Why would I be bothered about making love to you?" We had to be extremely quiet because my parents were in the house, so that was a problem, but I could never resist naked Ilya.

He chuckles softly, cupping my face. "Not what we did. What your father and I had to do."

I smile and place my hand on his. "Oh, no. I grew up with all of this, Ilya. I only worry about you not coming home to me."

"I'll always do my best to find my way back to you, either in this lifetime or the next." His mouth crushes mine. When he pulls away, he flips me onto my back and pins me to the mattress with my hands over my head. "Now, where were we? What concerns you?"

"When did you decide that you wanted to be with me?"

"That's tricky." He pauses and releases me, sitting up and lifting me onto his lap as he leans against his headboard. "I always cared for you. At first, it was as my godsister, and then I just loved to see you smile. Then, on your sweet sixteen, I couldn't stand anyone else dancing with you, so even though I shouldn't have, I took you onto the dance floor."

"Even then?"

"Yes, even then. It was wrong and I tried to push the feelings away, but I knew it was only a matter of time before I'd cave. Staying away was the best I could do for the both of us. Then you asked for a kiss. You have no idea how hard it was to force myself to just leave when all I wanted to do was take you right there."

"Funny, I've had a crush on you since I was ten years old and you picked me up after I fell off my bike. You carried me inside, got the first aid kit, and cleaned my cut knee like it was a must, as if none of our mothers were there to do the job."

"I've always felt protective over you in a way I can't even describe, in ways I wasn't with my siblings. So, I guess my love for you has been growing since we were young."

"I love you, Ilya."

"I'll love you forever, Natalya." We kiss, but just as we're about to go further, his alarm goes off. "Unfortunately, that means it's time for us to get up and get dressed."

"What are we doing today?"

"I have business matters to attend to, and you have to prepare for the wedding, including selecting your gown."

"Are you not going to be involved in any of the planning?"

"Not unless you want me to participate. I assure you that my mother and yours are probably going to be driving you nuts with all the decisions and questions." He pauses and tilts his head. "Do you want me to be there to intervene just in case they overstep?"

"Yes."

"Then I will work just this morning and move everything I can until later."

"Thank you."

"Anything for you." We kiss once more before getting dressed. "I'm so glad my father brought along my suitcases. I didn't pack everything I needed from your condo."

"It's our condo, and what do you need? I can get anything for you."

"It's fine. I just have my hairstyling products and makeup in my bags. If we're going places, I don't want these people to see me looking like a bum when I'm marrying someone like you."

"Someone like me? I'm marrying the most beautiful woman in the world."

"Thank you." I fix my hair and start putting on my makeup when there's a knock on the bedroom door.

Ilya goes to the door and opens it for my mother. "Good morning. Please come in. Natalya is still getting ready."

"I only came to let you both know that breakfast is ready and your father is starting to get growly, wondering where you are."

"I'm finished now." I roll my eyes and come out of the bathroom with my outfit and makeup completely done. "How do I look?"

"Like you are ready to take over the world," my mother says.

"Like I'm sending several extra guards with you today if you leave the estate. Better yet, I will accompany you."

"Actually, you can't. We're picking out her wedding gown today, so you will be doing something else."

"I guess today will be a good day to finish all your work."

"I suppose so, but I'm serious about your safety."

"I know." I reach up and kiss his cheek before walking out in front of him, shaking my ass.

"Don't worry, Ilya. We'll keep her safe and under control. No one will dare cross us."

"Thank you."

We enter the kitchen and my future father-in-law smiles at me, but my father is glaring at Ilya. "Took long enough this morning."

"Yes, well, some of us don't take five minutes to get dressed. I had to get pretty."

"You're already beautiful, sweetheart," my father says.

"I told you." Ilya kisses my hand and then goes to grab some coffee. "Would you like some, or would you prefer some orange juice?"

"Coffee," I groan. After our languid, quiet lovemaking, I slept like a baby, but it was still only six hours and I'm beat. He hands me a cup, and my mother-in-law slides over the serving tray of cream and sugar. I mix some in my coffee and then take a sip. It's freaking perfect and I let out a moan to prove it, which makes Ilya growl against my ear.

"Behave," he whispers. "Take a seat."

"So, are you heading into the office?" Mr. Semyonov asks Ilya.

"Yes, I have a lot to do and I'd like to make my presence known, just in case people get suspicious."

"We'll escort the ladies today."

"When is Junior coming?"

"I spoke to him this morning. He should be here before the wedding."

"What's he doing that he can't be here sooner?"

"That's not your concern, my little sweetling," my mother says, answering for my father.

"I hope it's not dangerous." From the look they're giving each other, I'm betting it's more than dangerous. It's deadly.

"I don't know why I bother asking. Anyway, I'd like some food before we go. I'm exhausted, and my body aches after yesterday."

"Excuse me, that's TMI," my other brother says.

"I'm talking about running from danger and being tied up, but..." Ilya covers my mouth.

"This wedding can't come soon enough."

CHAPTER
FOURTEEN

ILYA

IT'S my wedding day and I couldn't be happier, except my future brother-in-law isn't fucking here yet. He has a thing against me, but I thought that shit had ended. That fucking asshole is going to get murdered if he doesn't make it here before the ceremony starts.

"Where is he?" I snarl, staring at my father-in-law who looks equally worried. "Is there some transportation issue?" I add.

"Something like that."

"Natalya's going to be devastated if he's not here. I know the bastard has a thing against me."

"He doesn't. This has nothing to do with either of you —that is something I can promise. It's time for me to take my place and bring you your bride." He gives me a hug and then walks hurriedly down the aisle back to the bridal suite.

I believe he wouldn't hurt Natalya so I'm sure that Drago is telling me the truth, but it doesn't change the fact that her older brother isn't here when he promised he would be.

The music starts, and I take my place with my brother and Anatoly at my side. The side door of the church opens, and suddenly a little grumbling comes with a bit of shuffling. "You will sit and behave, or you won't sit right for the next couple of days," a loud hiss comes from Drago Romanov Jr. to a red-headed woman that he has braced by her elbow. She's in a pretty wedding outfit and wouldn't look out of place if it wasn't for the obvious handcuff on her wrist, linking her to Junior.

He's sporting a nice cut under his eye, and I wonder if she had anything to do with it. So this was the mission he was on. I doubt it had to do with bringing this woman here, but he's like his father.

"So glad you could make it," I say, addressing my brother-in-law while fighting off my smirk.

"I wouldn't miss my sister's wedding. Not even to an asshole like you."

"Flattery will get you nowhere." I wink and take my place because the doors open and my bride starts down the aisle.

She doesn't stop smiling as she reaches me on her father's arm, and then finally she looks to her side to see her brother. "You made it."

"Couldn't miss this important day."

"Thank you," she mouths.

Drago hands over my bride with his blessing, and the priest reads his prayers before saying our vows. Finally, it's the moment I've waited for, and I kiss my bride, dipping her in front of the entire crowd. My father-in-law coughs, and I set her on her feet properly.

"Let us welcome Mr. and Mrs. Ilya Semyonov." Even over the din of the celebratory cheers, I didn't miss the gasp coming from Junior's captive. I don't have time to ask because my time is for my bride, but I'm sure I'll learn more about my brother-in-law later about his little plus one before the night is over.

I watch her swim in the large pool at our private resort, a special honeymoon gift from my father. She looks so hot, but I have a call I must take, so I sit out on the deck and handle business. My eyes never leave my bride and her sexy figure in her blue bikini that hardly covers any of her assets. She glides through the water like a dolphin, making it appear effortless. I want to jump in behind her, but I have important business that can't wait. Grumbling to myself, sometimes I regret that I'm the heir to the Semyonov empire.

The words in front of me swim as my vision becomes distracted by the sudden appearance of a man on the property who is talking to my wife in the pool. I'm on my feet in a flash. "Mr. Semyonov, sorry, but no one answered the door."

"Then that means you don't come in at all," I say through clenched teeth, my fists balled up ready to bust his face.

"Don't be mean, Ilya. I ordered us lunch while you were busy." She lifts herself out of the pool, but I nudge her back in with just a look. She giggles, holding on to the edge of the pool while I take the bag from the young man and hand him a tip. As pissed as I am, he's aware of my obsession with my wife and the urge to destroy anyone who dares to take her from me.

"Keep walking." He scrams, and then I set the food down before lifting her out of the shallow end.

"Wife, are you trying to have me kill someone today?" I ask, dragging her to my body, not caring that my clothes will be wet. My body is heated.

"Sorry, I didn't want to disturb you. Besides, I was going to give him a tip." Her bag was on the chair near mine. She would have strutted nearly naked with water dripping down her soft, smooth skin in front of that bastard and I would have had to gouge his eyes out.

"You always disturb me." I press my palm on her ass, shoving her pussy against my cock. "He's lucky I let him walk away."

"Not everyone is interested in me."

"I'd like to agree, but a half-naked woman in a pool would be hard for a young man to ignore. Especially a woman who looks like you," I snarl. "His eyes were glued to you."

"I was speaking." I pop her wet ass.

"Don't argue with me, Wife, or I'll pull out the big guns."

"You better not call my father."

"Worse, I'll call your mother and she'll agree with me."

"Fine, you win. Still, it's time for me to eat. I have food for you, but if you're *too* busy to eat, I'll save your meal." She pulls out of my grasp and then walks toward her chair to snag the towel.

"No, I have time to eat, Princess." Is she pissed at me?

We step past the opened dual sliding doors, and I

help her set the food out on the round table meant for two. We eat, but there's a silence around it, and I can barely stomach the food, knowing that my woman is pissed. I set my fork down and sit back, staring at the love of my life. She eats, looking as if she doesn't have a care in the world, doing her best to ignore the fuck out of me.

My phone rings before I can bring up any conversation. "Go on, take it. It's probably important." I drop my phone on the table because the tone coming from her mouth answers all my fucking questions.

I reach across the table, taking her hand in mine that fights to take it back. "Sweetheart, love of my life, my heart and soul, do you feel neglected?"

"No..." I release her hand and push out of my chair in a flash. Within a second, I drag her chair back, grip the back of her hair, and tip her head upward as I lean down with my other palm flat on our table.

"Don't lie to me, Wife. Those pretty lips are telling me something different than what's going on in here." I run my hand over her heart, pressing firmly.

"You've worked every day that we've been here. This is supposed to be our honeymoon and not the time for you to be busy with anything else but me."

"I'm sorry, Princess. We probably should have waited to take our honeymoon until I had cleared up my schedule, but I promise that I'm done. Everything else will have to wait."

My phone rings again. "Don't make promises you can't keep. Just take the call."

"No. Nothing is as important as you. I want you to know that."

"Prove it, Mr. Semyonov." I grip my sexy wife's wrist

and lift her off the chair, flipping her ass onto the table. She bounces lightly, her tits doing the same thing.

"So sexy." My hands make quick work of the scraps of blue at her breasts. Fuck, they harden instantly from the cool breeze created from my movements, and my dick notices. "Wife, you have no idea how hard it has been to work with you nearby when all I want to do is slide in inside you, touch this precious skin, and run my fingers over your tender flesh, wondering how fast your pulse will quicken as I add my mouth." My hand skims along the column of her throat, my thumb pressing on her pulse.

"Ilya," she gasps, her pulse racing as I expected.

"Yes, Princess?"

"Somebody's watching us," she whispers.

I flip around and duck my wife to the floor and find a little child in the room. Quickly, I throw my jacket on my wife, who covers up. My gun is out, and I survey the area. The kid can't be more than three years old, but he couldn't have gotten in here without assistance. The area has been secured, unless that fucker who brought our food left the gate open. Still, security would have alerted us.

"Your phone." It rings again.

"Damn it." My phone had been ringing and I ignored it for so damn long, but I guess it was important. She hands it over.

It's my security. "Sir, the resort is on lockdown. Someone swiped the owner's child. They have him on camera, but he disappears somewhere near the beach around your villa. They're coming to question you."

"We have the boy. He's in our dining area, but I don't know where the kidnapper is."

"Come here, sweetie," Natalya says, bending down and sticking her arms out for him.

"Mama," he sobs. She takes him in her arms just as a bastard comes out of hiding. It's the guy who brought our food.

"You?"

"It's amazing how this all worked out in my favor. I get two for one. Kidnapping Cyprus King's heir and then killing him and leaving you to take the fall, a Russian piece of shit and his little whore of a wife."

"You're twice the fool because there's no way you're getting out of here alive." He goes for my wife, but I won't let anyone take her from me again. With a look at her, she knows the drill. She turns to the side, clutching the baby to her chest, and I quickly shoot the fucker in the head, sending him flying back, body hitting the floor.

The doors to the villa open, and several men enter with their guns pointed and ready to fire.

"Lower your fucking weapons in front of my wife and this small child," I roar. My men follow suit, and then I see Cyprus King eyeing the piece of shit against the wall and my wife cradling his baby. He orders his men to lower theirs.

"We presume this little one is yours?" Natalya asks.

"Hold on," I snarl. My wife isn't properly covered and if she hands over the baby, her covering is going to open, flashing a dozen men.

"Don't play games with me, Semyonov. Give me my son, or there will be hell to pay." The deadly look in his eyes meant business and normally, I wouldn't be intimidated by anyone and be enraged and his tone, but my wife is present and her life was more important to me than anything in the word. Protecting her is my ultimate priority, so I try to rein in my indignation.

I glare at him and put my hand up. "Calm down." Looking at my wife, I say, "Princess, come here." She complies with the baby, facing me. I take him so only I am graced with her sexy breasts. "Go and put some clothes on."

"Oh," King says, the compromising situation sorting itself out.

"Yes. I'd hate to have to cut all their eyes out. So here is your little man." He takes his son and presses him firmly to his chest. I can see he's fighting tears in his eyes, but at the moment he's remaining strong.

"I can't thank you enough for this." He sticks out one hand while holding his boy firmly with the other.

I shake it. "It was just chance. Who the hell is this prick ruining my honeymoon?"

"I'm not sure. He works for the food services. My wife was hungry and ordered something for her and the baby. I was busy working when everything went down. My wife is with the medical team now."

"Shit." If I hadn't been sitting by the pool, he might have tried to harm Natalya. Speaking of her, she comes out in a pretty dress.

"Hello, cutie," she coos. He reaches for her, but his father holds on to him tightly.

"Sorry," King apologizes for the overreaction.

"Don't worry. I'm not offended. I can't imagine someone trying to kidnap our children."

"We thank you, but I must take him to his mother.

She is worried, and I don't want her to get worse. Also, you can have your belongings prepared and the resort staff will move you to another villa."

"What about this piece of shit?" I kick his fucking boot, wanting him to still be alive so I could kill him again. The thought that he was willing to hurt my wife was sending my blood racing through my veins like a violent tidal wave. All I could think of was murdering someone. Finding who sent the fucker was important to me even if it was to get at King. His enemy was now mine.

"We'll dispose of him, and then find out who he's working with and deal with them as well."

"Keep me informed. He knew who we were and wanted us gone as well."

"I will." He and his men leave the villa. Looking to my men, I give a command. "Secure this area. If anyone gets in, it's your heads. Understood?" They nod and reply with the affirmative. They take their orders and leave the area while I lead my wife to our room.

"Ilya, I need you right now."

I lift her up and carry her to the bathroom. After what happened, I don't want any interruptions. Turning on the shower, I tear off her dress, tossing it on the floor before kissing down her body, licking her breasts. I don't bother getting all the way undressed because I need to have her. "You're mine, Natalya. You belong to me," I grunt, stuffing my length deep into her tight pussy with a single thrust. My hands plant on the granite counter while my dick pierces her womb.

"Yes, oh my God."

"God's going to need his eyes closed on this one." My dick slides out and then I ram it back in, hearing her grunt from the fullness. Wrapping my fingers around her thighs, I hold them and plunge faster and rougher, every stroke demanding, taking her pussy violently and needing to reassure us both that we're one. I fuck her tiny hole until she claws down on my chest.

"Do you know how fucking hot you look taking my dick?"

"No."

"It's time you saw." I pull out and flip her to face the mirror. With her knees bent and her hands splayed on the mirror, I slide back in from behind. "Look how sexy you are taking your husband's big cock."

"Oh, Ilya, don't stop. I'm going to come all over your massive cock. Give it to me."

"Fuck, baby. Take that dick like the slutty little wife you are. You like seeing yourself being fucked so hard, don't you?" She nods, but that's not good enough. With a growl, I fist her hair. "I didn't hear you, my princess."

"Yes, my ruthless prince. Fuck me hard." My muscles flex as I hold her tight, drilling her tiny body. I'm so close to nutting that I need her to come. My hand slips down, and I strum that little fucking pearl while my sweet wife sings my name. "I'm coming, Ilya. Ilya. Ilya."

"So am I." I flood her walls with ropes of my seed, painting her pussy with cum until I've got nothing left. I'll never get tired of draining myself inside her, marking her with my release, staking my claim. Then I set her on her feet and lean on her back as we both catch our breath. "You're mine for the rest of our days and the next life, Natalya." I brush my lips against her throat.

"Now that's what I'm talking about. All it took was offing some dude."

"No, you were about to get fucked on the table like this earlier, but we were interrupted. I missed my appetizer before the main course."

"Pity. I can freshen up, and I'll save your dessert for later."

"Sounds good. We do have some packing to do, and you know that makes me hungry." She jumps in the shower, and I watch the erotic show in front of me, forgetting everything else because my wife is sexy as hell, and honestly there's nothing I want to do more than spend time admiring her.

A text hit my phone an hour later.

The asshole was the last of the Fratelli heirs.

I don't give two fucks about any of Fratelli's kids. I just offed his son, and I'll take out any others that come for my family. Luckily, their empire is crumbling and there isn't anyone willing to risk their lives for those fucking losers. The dumb bitches who had been helping them had found themselves in trouble. That Jordan chick ended up overdosing two weeks ago in a motel. Rachel ended up on the FBI's radar and cut a deal to point out some of Nico Fratelli's allies.

I need a list of those bastards myself just in case.

"Are you ready, Ilya?" Natalya says, sliding her arms around my waist.

"Yes, yes."

"Something's on your mind," she insists, tipping her head up and pressing her chin into my chest. I run my hand down her back and to her ass, cupping her plump cheeks. "Don't distract me, husband."

"I'm not. I love you and I'm thinking about your

safety. I don't want to be complacent about it. King was and it nearly cost him his family."

"I'm sure you won't. Don't forget to tell our parents about the attack today." I stare down at her in amazement because I expect her to want this washed away and definitely hidden from her father. "What? I'm your wife now. You have been raised to be ruthless and I'm not stopping you."

"I'm about to fuck you again, princess."

"As soon as we get to our other room. Now, finish packing." She slaps my ass and runs away. I love that woman and get to work because our new room must be christened. "You're going to pay for that," I call out.

She leans back into the room. "Counting on it." She winks from the bedroom door, spanking her ass and then dashes away while giggling. Shaking my head, I take care of what I need to do before hunting down my bride.

By the time we leave the resort, I know two things: we added another ally and destroyed an enemy.

EPILOGUE

NATALYA

THE MAN I married stares me down across the yard at my parents' home during a pool party. The dark look across his light eyes is a warning, laced with intent. A smirk crosses my face as I think about the first time I crossed that line with him. God, it was so many years ago. With two children and a third on the way, which he doesn't know about, I can't believe how horny I am as he watches me. It's my sister's birthday and it's a big deal to her, but all I can think about is the devil staring at me.

"Lord, could you two get a room?" my mother's voice comes from directly behind me.

"Mother," I gasp, turning toward her. She smiles at me because my father hasn't changed in all their years. With all their children, you'd think they didn't have time to fool around, but they only came back outside to the party five minutes ago. He's just as unsettled about the guests as Ilya, but for different reasons. "We have a room. If you'll excuse us and keep an eye on the boys, I need to discuss something with my grumpy husband."

"Yes, before he crushes someone's skull." Yes, today there's a lot of younger men invited to the party for my sister because she attended a regular high school. My father hates having all these young bucks around his little girl.

Ilya doesn't like the way they're staring at me. I can't say I blame him because the girls are practically giggling when they see him. Nothing has changed when it comes to girls and my husband. He's hot, and they lose their minds.

I saunter into the kitchen, taking a paper towel and leaning over the kitchen island to wipe it off.

"Mrs. Semyonov," Ilya snarls in my ear, stepping behind me the moment I'm completely bent over. "Are you trying to get someone killed today, or get thoroughly fucked?"

"I'm trying to stop the first and enjoy the second." His bulge is firmly pressed against my ass and if he could, he'd slide his cock deep inside me right on the spot. "Someone could come in here at any moment."

"Then we better take this somewhere else because I'm not ready to head back out there." That I'm sure of. Ilya's itching to destroy someone and I'd rather it be my pussy than some little punk's face.

"Sexcuse me," I say, bumping him with my ass before I run up the stairs like a silly teenager chasing after Ilya, but instead, this time he's the one on my heels.

We sneak into the guest bedroom where we're staying this time. My old bedroom has been turned into a nursery for all the grandbabies. "This room looks awfully familiar," he says, staring me down.

I pressed my hand to his shirt, tapping my fingernails on his chest. "Yes, I do recall a gentleman accosting me in here a few years back."

"Oh really?" He looks at my fingers and then grasps my hand, stilling my movements. "What happened with this gentleman?"

"Yes. See...he dared me to flaunt my pussy in front of him again." I lick my lips.

"Well, what are you waiting for?" He steps back and creates some distance between us, lowering his gaze to my core.

I cross my arms and stare at the man I've loved for so many years and toss out my own challenge. "I think I've shown it to you plenty of times, my godbrother. You should show me your big bat."

"Dirty little godsister, on your knees." I smile and drop in front of him, something I've done so many times before but never in this room in my parents' house. "Fuck, so perfect. Now be a good girl and take out my dick." I do what he demands, unbuckling his pants and unleashing his massive cock.

I take his lengthy girth in my hands, stroking it up and down from base to tip, watching it get harder and the tip glisten with a bead of precum. "Don't be a tease. You wanted it, now take it," he commands, voice shaking with need. I love the way he comes undone by my touch.

"Will you buy me another pretty necklace?"

"Keep it up, and I'll give you a necklace right now." His hand wraps around my throat, and my pussy squirts a little. Slamming my thighs together, I take him in my mouth, moaning and slobbering as I enjoy his massive cock.

I never get tired of watching him lose control.

"Fuck, you're going to make me come, and that's not going to work for me." I pop my lips off his rod and ask, "Why not?"

He lifts me onto my feet and rushes me over to the bed where he bends me over and tosses my dress over my back, running his hands over my ass. A swift smack comes down on my bottom, causing me to yelp before I let out a moan. "Because I want my load dripping down your thighs so every man can smell me on you. I want you fucked so hard you step outside walking funny so that every dickhead knows you're taken."

"Like the ring and the children running around aren't signs enough?"

"No, that's not enough," he growls, shoving my panties down my legs. He's quick as he lifts one leg onto the bed and then slides into me. I gasp from the fullness, pressing my hands on the bed for support. "No, Princess." He takes my arms and pulls them to my sides, bracing them as he fucks me hard. His chest presses against my back, holding me close as he drills into me. I cry out, aching with pleasure as he takes me rough.

"Yes, Ilya. Yes."

"Who do you belong to, Natalya?"

"You. I belong to you. Always."

"Good wife," I answer. His mouth latches onto my throat, sucking until I come undone.

He roars his own release, filling me up with so much that I'm sure I'll be a mess. He tilts my head and kisses my lips. "I love you so much, my sexy godsister."

"To think I had to chase you down to get a kiss."

"That's because you were too young for me. Like you said all those years ago—it wasn't that I didn't want to kiss you." He kisses me again, and we ignore the knocking that comes from the door.

"Mommy, Grandma says you have to tell Daddy to help. Papa pushed someone in the pool."

"Damn it."

"Daddy is on his way."

"Don't let him drown," I insist. He kisses me hard and fast before rushing out the door. "You can handle the problem later." Smiling, he does just that. Some fools never learn that you can't mess with Bratva royalty.

ABOUT THE AUTHOR

Find out more about Carina Blake:
Website: www.carinablake.com
Facebook: www.facebook.com/AuthorCarinaBlake
Instagram: www.facebook.com/AuthorCarinaBlake
Tiktok: www.tiktok.com/@carinablake
Bookbub: www.bookbub.com/profile/carina-blake
Works:

ALSO BY CARINA BLAKE

www.ingramcontent.com/pod-product-compliance
Lightning Source LLC
Chambersburg PA
CBHW051923240626
47153CB00004B/1342